A Home Subscription! It's the easiest and most convenient way to get every one of the exciting Coventry Romance Novels! ...And you get 4 of them FREE!

You pay nothing extra for this convenience; there are no additional charges...you don't even pay for postage! Fill out and send us the handy coupon now, and we'll send you 4 exciting Coventry Romance novels absolutely FREE!

SEND NO MONEY, GET THESE
FOUR BOOKS
FREE!

━━ ━━ ━━ ━━ ━━ ━━ ━━ ━━ ━━ ━━ ━━ ━━ ━━

C0181

MAIL THIS COUPON TODAY TO:
COVENTRY HOME
SUBSCRIPTION SERVICE
6 COMMERCIAL STREET
HICKSVILLE, NEW YORK 11801

YES, please start a Coventry Romance Home Subscription in my name, and send me FREE and without obligation to buy, my 4 Coventry Romances If you do not hear from me after I have examined my 4 FREE books, please send me the 6 new Coventry Romances each month as soon as they come off the presses. I understand that I will be billed only $10.50 for all 6 books There are no shipping and handling nor any other hidden charges. There is no minimum number of monthly purchases that I have to make. In fact, I can cancel my subscription at any time. The first 4 FREE books are mine to keep as a gift, even if I do not buy any additional books

For added convenience, your monthly subscription may be charged automatically to your credit card.

☐ Master Charge   ☐ Visa

Credit Card # _____

Expiration Date _____

Name _____
Please Print

Address _____

City _____ State _____ Zip _____

Signature _____

☐ Bill Me Direct Each Month

An Affair
of Dishonour

AUDREY BLANSHARD

FAWCETT COVENTRY • NEW YORK

AN AFFAIR OF DISHONOUR

This book contains the complete text of the original hardcover edition.

Published by Fawcett Coventry Books, a unit of CBS Publications, the Consumer Publishing Division of CBS Inc., by arrangement with Robert Hale Limited

ISBN: 0-449-50152-3

Printed in the United States of America

First Fawcett Coventry printing: January 1981

10 9 8 7 6 5 4 3 2 1

One

Humphrey Freen stared fixedly through the near window of the diligence. Outside, more of the alien countryside of Northern France passed his jaundiced eye, as background to the colourful spectacle of the huge-booted and rascally postillion riding near the wheel horses. Wearily he looked back inside the huge clumsy coach at his score or so of equally alien travelling companions—with the exception of Sam Mayhew, of course, dozing beside him.

The Earl of Begbroke and heir to the Marquisate of Cornford was a very tall fair-haired youth whose dress was habitually rather unfashionable and rustic even in his own country; abroad that effect was more marked. The Earl, together with the Reverend Samuel Mayhew, had left Calais three days previously after enduring a sea crossing whose rigours would have made even his irate father feel remorse; or so Humphrey tried to believe. His own twenty-four-year-old frame had suffered harshly enough, while as for the middle-aged family chaplain, he had looked and acted like a ghost ever since.

The mercy of reaching dry land again had not otherwise afforded much relief to the two Tourists. For once borne bodily ashore by the exorbitant Calais watermen, and after undergoing a more official stripping at the Custom House, yet another obstacle had still to be encountered.

The set and savage wind which had held them so long from port had finally relented only after the tide was out and the town gate closed against them; hence their need for row-boats, the services of the watermen, and finally a night's lodging at a ramshackle boarding-house outside Calais itself.

In any event the pair were hardly in prime twig by then to sample the renowned sea crabs of Quillac's Hotel. Both had crawled exhausted into their oddly high and overpadded French beds at the boarding-house, and risen rather late from them the next morning to explore the town.

That was when Humphrey's sombre spirits had sunk still lower as he gazed about him. Unwilling though he was to undertake the Tour, and still feeling battered through-and-through after the long hours of sea-sickness, even so he would have been fairminded enough to acknowledge Calais as a decent enough French town—if that was what it was.

What he had in fact looked upon, that first spring morning of his exile, was something even worse than Dover where they had waited upon the weather before boarding the packet. For whereas Dover had been merely sad and squalid, with its forest of inn-signs and population of poor old broken-down sailors, Calais struck him forcibly as being of a different order of meanness altogether.

It was indeed a curious place. At first the locals had seemed not unintriguing, with some instances of what appeared to be Anglo-Saxon features and colouring in evidence amongst the swarthiness he was braced to find. "Deuced odd, these fair fellows, are they not?" Humphrey had asked the Chaplain curiously as they wandered along.

The latter gentleman, despite his extreme morning pallor, was the usual mine of boring information.

"Let me think, my lord . . . Oh yes. I collect it was Edward the—most certainly *one* of the Edwards who captured this town and, ahem, shall we say *induced* many of its inhabitants to remove elsewhere. Legend has it that our own militia then undertook to remedy the deficiency," he said with his customary delicacy of expression.

"Ah, sir, that would account for it." Humphrey, reassured by this explanation, risked a half-smile back at one of the jovial group of men (well-built for French) who were just then passing them, dressed in their outlandish uniforms. "At least they do not seem inclined to molest us," he observed *sotto voce* to the Chaplain.

"Oh no, my lord: their Bonapartes may come and go but mercenary matters are ever first with them."

Calais itself had exceeded the Earl's very worst forebodings of foreign crudity. It had made even Dover seem to him like a last dear memory of home.

For apart from Quillac's, Meurice's, and the English-owned and recommended Lion d'Argent— which last they had failed to reach upon arrival due to the absurd and Gothick business of the lowering of the gate—this entry point to the European Continent seemed to consist of no more than a rubbishing seaside village. Although Mr. Mayhew had suggested they pause there for a day to recuperate, his charge had insisted that they leave betimes on the public coach.

At the outset of their journey the apprehensive cleric had enjoined his own polite entreaties to Humphrey's impassioned ones that they should be permitted to take a family carriage with them to the Continent; but the head of the House of Freen had been adamant. "You are fortunate, in the regrettable circumstances of your departure, to be upon wheels at all," he had informed his son, in a tone of arctic restraint which still resounded in Humphrey's ears. And the Marquis had taken unnatural pains to see his heir deprived of sufficient funds for the hiring of private equipages to be undertaken while he was out of England—save only in the direst circumstances. Indeed his father made no bones of wishing to punish rather than improve him by means of this cultural experience; and knowing Humphrey's plain and insular nature as well as he did, that intent seemed likely to be gratified.

Certainly the rough construction of the diligence, and its mob of mixed humanity, would have met with his entire approval to that end. For if it rested upon springs at all they were unfelt; its passengers all faced the front like a voluble French congregation; and the stench of garlic hung thickly in the atmosphere and defied the fresh air beyond the open windows.

But it was the ready conversation of the travelling French which had particularly startled and disgusted the young nobleman. For though his experience with his native public coaches was limited—confined, in fact, to a few revel-routs on the Mail with young Kentish friends—he was aware enough of the customary reserve of his fellow-countrymen while en route in this way as to be appalled by the constant chatter of these French. Moreover, unsure though his command of the language still was, he suspected that much which they forced him to overhear in this manner was quite improper; in several instances passengers who had given every early sign of being total strangers to one another (and sometimes of the opposite sex) were soon talking and laughing together in a style that he could only heartily deplore.

Conversely, when they halted at the many poor inns on their way south towards Paris, an equally surprising silence would descend upon the company.

For these French, it seemed, would prose together at the drop of a hat; but it was also their odd custom to munch away at the over-cooked *table d'hôte* fare served to them almost as mutely as the seven horses of the diligence consumed their fortifying oats.

The latter animals were changed very frequently, so that in fact quite a cracking pace was being sustained all the way to the Capital. But this reflection did little to alter Humphrey's now settled gloom.

The coach had disgorged a few people at the stops en route and picked up replacements: a group of flagrant Papists at Bernet, with tinkling little bells up their sleeves; some vulgar fellow-English whom he was ashamed of at Amiens; and a family of seven females had joined at Beauvais whose fluency with both languages led him to suppose that they must be at least half-French, if not entirely so. Their added presence he found uncomfortable in a way that he could not quite fathom. Though their party was seated nearby he had given only the stiffest acknowledgment to the tentative smile of the matron in charge. His eyes took in the fact that her brood was mostly pretty, but his sombre mind received that intelligence unmoved.

So now he was somewhat startled when, towards St Denis and nearing the end of this first stage of his Continental banishment, one of the young ladies of that group addressed him suddenly and calmly: "To be sure, sir, I have never seen such a Friday face as yours! At least, not one that I can recall!"

The first moments of embarrassment turned quickly to hot-faced annoyance on Humphrey's part. To be spoken to so—and by a young woman whose English accent lay in some indeterminate region between his own and the Frogs' . . . This was beyond anything!

He began to say in his starchiest manner: "I do not believe, ma'am, that I—" but she cut in with an impatient snort: "Of course you haven't! You haven't put yourself out to meet anyone about you, and make it very clear you feel not the least desire to do so!"

Humphrey's gaze slid away from her—a trifle desperately—to Sam Mayhew beside him. But the still ailing and exhausted clergyman remained fast asleep, the round chin of his round face nodding on his breast-bone, oblivious of his new duties as bear-leader.

Humphrey cleared his throat in a manner that attempted to convey his sense of outrage. But—since that procedure did not of itself suggest a single word to say to this pushing creature—he found himself rapidly losing still more countenance while his mind ran over various crushing setdowns; none of which, however, seemed quite apt for this occasion.

Whilst doing so he noticed vaguely that this assailant upon his privacy was dressed in a dark red travelling pelisse. Her hair was nearly black, which he attributed at once to French blood, and her large eyes, also, seemed over-dark to be pure English under their sharply-defined brows. But her complexion was reassuringly pink and cream, and she wore a hat with a high wagon-tilt poke similar to the absurd confections which he had lately seen upon his sisters' heads in Kent. Her hair was vulgarly crimped, her nose small and up-turned. Apart from its present line of mocking impudence, her mouth was well-shaped and perhaps a shade voluptuous; he recalled her now as the big eater of her family—the one who as a rule ate voraciously of every daunting dish set before them in the wayside hostelries, though her figure betrayed no signs of this indulgence and indeed she was slightly skinny.

"You are French, I collect?" he enquired, in a way that was at once half-accusatory and half-hesitant. For in truth he did not know where he was with her at all.

Again this remark elicited an unladylike snort. "No, why should I be?"

"Then I must congratulate you upon your command of their tongue."

"Oh, as to that I have lived here for a time, and also I have Miss de la Chêne to thank." She stuck out a finger baldly across the coach at an unsmiling female who wore a black bombazine dress ruffed at the neck and who, when Humphrey glanced at her directly, he could see was indeed the unmistakable governess of the party. Once again, as he looked over there, he received a lazy smile of approval from the lady in black whom he took to be the girls' parent; and who appeared entirely easy that one daughter was addressing and pestering him. It seemed the whole family was lost to conduct—though less offensively—as the other party of noisy English who had boarded the coach at Amiens.

It suddenly came to him that there was a simple enough means at hand for him to deliver a set-down; though not one which came at all naturally to him, since he was never one to place himself on too high a form under normal, unprovoked circumstances. "The

Earl of Begbroke, your servant . . ." he drawled insufferably. (Just as Hipsley himself might have uttered the words, he reflected, before the thought of That Name fetched the usual red mist across his eyes.)

"Beg what? Oh, I guessed you must be another such," was the unabashed reply. "I made the acquaintance of a brace of earls this day sennight, whilst Mama was taking us to look over the abbey at Mortagne. One had grown the new whiskers and the other's hair put me in mind of a Friesland hen. They were dead bores, both!"

With Humphrey again bereft of speech she rattled on: "We learned the strangest thing! The monks in the abbey there are vowed to perpetual silence. I should think that must be a dead bore too, wouldn't you?"

"I hazard that you would find it so," he responded, with a devastating Hipsley lip-curl; but this feeble condescension also passed quite unheeded by her.

"Where are you and the old man bound for? Oh, I am Anne Thouvenal, if I did not say so before."

"Aha, so you are French," he pronounced with dour satisfaction. Much of his sense of outrage melted away as he thus lowered her station in his mind.

"No, although our Papa was."

"A good enough reason," he observed dryly.

"Well, yes and no: it is *complicated,* you see. Our Papa was killed while he was fighting for the Emperor. Before that, for a while, we all lived with him here in France near Lyons. Then we returned once more to dear old Lincolnshire, where *some* of my sisters were born, and of course Mama herself originally. We are on our way now to search for our Papa's grave in Spain. Poor Mama is twice widowed, you see. Her first was our *English* papa, you see. My elder sisters there are not fully mine, you see . . ."

But Humphrey was 'seeing' very little of this embarrassing and incoherent rush of confidence, as he cast a further haughty stare at the sizable group of whole or part-Thouvenals in the coach. He was also smarting at the revelation that, quite unwittingly, he had been entrapped into conversing with an actual relation to one of the Monster's soldiery. Her precious Elban Emperor, indeed! He uttered a snort not unlike the young lady's own habitual prelude to conversation as he tried to think of something positively annihilating to say to her.

But none of his responses seemed to affect or concern her in the slightest. She was now continuing: "Before Papa, Mama was wed to an Englishman, as I said. He was the father of my two sisters there, sitting under the band-boxes. (Again that vulgar jabbing forefinger.) But he died, and then Mama wed *my* Papa, and we all lived with him until the war started and he sent us home to England again, as I said, and—"

"Just so," Humphrey interrupted faintly. He was not in fact a stupid young man, merely one who had temporarily drawn in upon himself due to the harshness of fate, and a suspicion was now belatedly coming to him that despite this chit's mature appearance and ways, there was a certain underlying juvenility to her prattle which . . . "How old are you?" he demanded, with a peremptoriness of manner which would have been impossible for him to adopt without having suffered her previous blurted remarks.

"Fifteen," she told him brightly. "This is my second visit to the Continent. I collect it is but your first, my lord?"

To be condescended by a schoolroom miss in disguise! This discovery was the final straw! Humphrey glowered down at the French mud on his top boots.

"Why *have* you come abroad? One can see that you wish yourself otherwhere every second," she persisted with her unsnubbable childish curiosity.

"To make the Tour, why else?" he ground out.

She laughed piercingly in his ear. "I had little need to ask as to that!" She gestured at Humphrey's and Mr Mayhew's extensive baggage, bouncing overhead with the other passengers' on the large network suspended from the roof. "But what other reason besides?" She regarded him now with a shrewdness which belied her years more than had any of the previous talk between them.

To his no small astonishment, the dejected young nobleman found that he was glad of the chance to unburden himself to this stranger. (Perhaps the impulse came to him just because she was a stranger —and a devilish odd one at that, in his opinion. But in only a few more miles they would reach Paris and, no doubt, part for evermore. She thus made an ideal person to hear the tale of his abject disgrace which, unbeknownst to him, he had been longing to reveal to some uninvolved listener ever since the morning of the duel.)

"Because I was called out," he mumbled slowly, looking far-away through the coach window.

"*Called out!* How famous! But surely a trifle quaint? Oh, I do not doubt your word—I can picture you enacting it only too well! And which place in the wilds was the scene of this outmoded affair? Cornwall? Scotland? Did you contest it with a sword?"

Her loud laugh ran again through the coach; then cut off short when she looked at his face again. In a changed tone she said: "I did not mean to roast you . . . A duel for what reason? For a woman?"

"I wish to God that it had been for so customary and intelligible a reason!" Humphrey burst forth. He dug his fingers into one of the close-by little leather pockets in the lining of the diligence where travellers deposited their bread and snuff and night-caps. He plucked forth a morsel of bread now, and chewed it, without thinking or tasting.

"In Kent, with pistols," he murmured at last, answering her former pert questions with a hollow gravity which finally subdued even the precocious Miss Thouvenal. Her lively curiosity, however, was now fully aroused.

"Yes, but *why*?" she demanded, in a ringing tone which for a moment stilled the hubbub in the rest of the coach.

Humphrey Freen uttered a harsh chuckle through his bread-crumbs. Spluttering slightly, he told her: "You ask me why—I will tell you why . . . Because I was luckless enough and witless enough to break the leg of a gentleman of reputation, that is why!"

She stared open-mouthed, dark eyes now serious but still alight with her former teasing humour.

"A *gentleman of reputation*? I had not the slightest notion that any such creatures were still in existence!"

Humphrey gave her a wan smile. "No more had I, a short while ago. But you may take my word on it that one such specimen is still very much alive and thriving."

Again his bitterness impressed Anne Thouvenal, and she was silent as he began to sketch to her the chapter of accidents which had led him so inexorably to that fateful early morning near Canterbury. "I should make it known to you at the outset, ma'am, that I am not one who is by nature over-inclined toward the bottle," he began in pompous tones; but to that claim Miss Thouvenal merely snorted her snort and adjured him:

"Pray proceed to the meat of the matter—remember, we journey together only until Paris—not Moscow like the Emperor! I declare I detest nothing more on this earth than an abandoned tale just when one is deep in it!"

". . . No, not from inclination a drinker in the least degree, he continued morosely, not listening to her at all now that his mind was gripped back in the vice of the past. "But on that particular occasion—only once, mind . . ." He winced, smoothing his straight-cut yellow locks aside with a clenched fist.

"On one occasion, then, you were as drunk as a wheelbarrow," Miss Thouvenal prompted briskly.

He shrugged, smiling despite himself. None of his sisters—irritating though they sometimes were—had ever spoken to him in such a forthright fashion. He found it not altogether displeasing (once over the surprise) and it did seem to help him, somehow, to give an account of his present wretchedness.

"It was the night of my birthday," he said more evenly.

"Your twenty-first?" she asked, idly searching his face.

"You lag by three years."

"Oh: you seem—I mean, you look younger." Even Miss Thouvenal, it seemed, did not dispense with tact entirely.

"As I say—if you will kindly not interrupt me—I celebrated to the point of unwisdom, whilst out with some friends on that curst night.

"*That curst night!*" she exclaimed delightedly. Humphrey's mode of expression appeared to amuse her in a way that he could not fathom; and indeed he thought it shocking in the grave circumstances he was describing. He glowered at her in fresh resentment until she told him: "Oh, pay no mind to me, my lord. I assure you I most sincerely wish to hear what you have to say!"

She regarded him in a way that oozed sympathy but which also, he felt dimly, made him out to be a clunch. But he was by now too engrossed with his memories to draw back from them on her account. "We made eight that evening, in all . . ."

"Out on the town in Canterbury, you say?" (For her promise to keep silent was plainly mere rhetoric.)

"No, Miss Thouvenal, on that occasion it was at Tunbridge Wells."

"Good—that much we have now established, then: eight young Kentish Bloods of the First Stare (her lips quivered slightly), all in drink, in Tunbridge Wells, on your birthday. *And then?*"

"Then we became quarrelsome," Humphrey muttered.

"A consequence which does not entirely astound me."

He gave a faint frown with his colourless brows, bewildered by her irony when his own thoughts were so different. "Tom Berry egged the rest of us on . . . he downed twelve pints . . . though strangely he was not the most foxed by half . . . I myself had only seven," he finished aggrievedly. For it still rankled with him that the merchant Berry's roistering and capacious son had faced no duel, and no prolonged nightmare, ensuing from that night's indulgence whereas he—He shook off that petty resentment with a sigh.

A small foot stamped hard beside his on the coach floor.

"Oh, don't start feeling hipped again, just when it becomes almost interesting! What *happened* out of this quarrel you speak of? How did a few brangling boys, however sapskulled and drunken, become involved with an affair of honour—as I believe it was once termed?"

But the young lady's sharp tongue had lashed him once too often; in his deliberate and plodding way, Humphrey now broke off his story in an attempt to give her some insight into what his life had been like before the events which he was about to describe. He felt that some background was needed to engage her sympathy as well as her interest; or perhaps it was nearer to the truth that he simply seized the chance to postpone giving himself the pain of re-living the course of that fatal chance meeting with Hipsley. (For by now he was fast realising that it meant more dulled pain, as well as some relief, to rake over the near past in this way with a stranger.)

He made an effort to convey to her what his ordinary, but to him very pleasant life in the country had meant to him: how he had declined to go up to Oxford when younger, on the ground that he had little love of learning but a very real interest in managing the estate; also a shrewd suspicion that he was good for only a Master of Arts at university, and no taken degree; of his father's final reluctant acceptance of that decision; of his subsequent period of near-total peace and contentment until he first laid eyes on Lydia Richardson of East Sussex; of her rejection of his suit in favour of another, and his then turning back to boyhood friends for a companionship which, in maturity, they were ill-placed to supply. (Several having dropped the handkerchief themselves by that time, or become lovelorn likewise—a condition which, he soon learned, grew no easier to bear for being compounded.)

And so gradually he returned, by way of this half-informative and half-evasive path, to Tunbridge Wells and the exact circumstances in which Major Guy Hipsley of the Dragoon Guards had fractured his fibula there.

— Two

But after finally explaining the facts of the matter to Miss Thouvenal, he knew what she was likely to ask him next, and realised that his honest answer to that question must convince her beyond any doubt that he was a well-born natural, travelling abroad with a culpably inattentive keeper.

His fears were soon realised. "What did this man Hipsley look like when you first noticed him in the ale-house? I should have supposed that such a person would appear dangerous enough, without the point being tested."

Humphrey bared his teeth in a resigned and humourless grimace. "I daresay that was so, had I noticed him at all—had I seen him at all."

She gaped like the schoolgirl she really still was. "Not *seen* him? Not *seen the man whose leg you broke*?"

Silently he shook his head at her. "Alas, no. I am aware that it sounds havey-cavey in the extreme, but to this day I have not the slightest recollection of seeing Guy Hipsley's face, or of assaulting his person, at that wretched inn! The news of it only reached me later, in this fashion . . ."

He went on to describe how, early the next morning, he had strolled to a coffee-house under the Music Balcony in the Pantiles, there to meet by prior arrangement one Richard Masterson, who had been among their party the night before. He, Humphrey, had felt surprisingly well and light-hearted that fine spring morn, and unaccountably free from any lingering symptoms of indulgence. Not so his friend Richard; and at first he had attributed the latter's air of strain entirely to that likely consequence. The detail of their talk had run along a course which time had already fogged—although the substance of the exchange was unlikely ever to be forgotten by either of them.

He had begun in cheerful tones: "Ah, Dick! My God, you look fierce today! And yet you downed less than me, you dog! What shall—"

"Don't concern yourself on my head," Dick Masterson had said in an odd, shaky voice. "Sit down." And, once that suggestion was complied with: "Pray, what *are you going to do*, Humph?"

"I? Do?" The Earl had responded, startled by his friend's intensity of manner. "Why, I am of a disposition to be fixed here a day or two more, I think. 'Tis a pleasant enough town and one almost unknown to me—tho' I seem to recall an old aunt of ours has a place a few miles north towards Sevenoaks—that's if she ain't cut her stick without my noticin'! While I'm here I may call on her and—I say, old fellow, are you feeling half as bad as you seem? You were primed from the same hogshead as the rest of us, weren't you, Dicky? Are the others in the same queer stirrups as you?" (And, as he recalled, an idiotish grin of pride in his own superior constitution had spread over his features as he said that.)

"You *aunt?*" Dick Masterson repeated, staring with his protuberant eyes. "You can just sit there, twirling a spoon and talking of your *aunt ...?*" Words seemed to fail him at that juncture.

Humphrey had misunderstood him. "I assure you my aunt is a perfectly respectable connexion," he declared with a certain chilly *hauteur*. Since, dash it, if one was facing facts, Dicky Masterson was no more than a second son. Fond of him though he was, it did rather set him on his high ropes, whether Dicky was indisposed or not, that one should have to listen to him disparaging on Ingram.

Humphrey's expression must have at last conveyed to his drinking companion that they were more than slightly at loggerheads. He decided to lose no further time in coming to the point. In a hoarse and stageish whisper he told him: "Hipsley still keeps his rooms by Lower Walk!"

When Humphrey's countenance remained a blend of annoyance and blankness, Richard rose to his feet in a nervous bound, knocking over the coffee-table so that their cups and saucers bounced and spilled over on the polished boards. "Humph!—whilst you sit here raving about calling on your aunt—Hipsley has called *you out!*"

"Eh? Who has? What?"

"Guy Hipsley!" Richard almost choked in strangled tones.

"I know the name," Humphrey allowed musingly, but still without any real degree of comprehension.

"I should suppose that you do! For I hazard everyone in England knows that name by now! Humph, they say he has killed *nine!*—and been out as many more times! One of the nine being the victim of that wild caper in Shropshire two years back, when they shot from cover-hacks at ten yards! Humph, you must have your cattle put to *this instant,* and bedamned to your breakfast! For that man is no less than *murderous*—without his passions being engaged as they are now! They say he is half-mad with pain and rage and, over all, humiliation, and is resolved to settle it before you can leave here! All that holds him back is the sawbone's tardiness in rigging the splint to bear his weight! For God's sake—quit the Wells now!"

In his vehemence, the bulging-eyed Masterson had now produced a gold pick and was jabbing with it recklessly amongst his rather forward-set teeth. Most of his features tended towards over-prominence, although the total effect was surprisingly pleasant.

"But why should I, Dick?" asked the Earl in the deepest bewilderment. "What am I supposed to have done to incur this person's wrath? What *is* all this fustian you're talking? I truly do not understand you!"

Whereupon Masterson had flung his head back and positively brayed: "Why, man, you broke Hipsley's leg! You threw him in a kind of cross-butt, clear over the ale-draper's shelf! He fell . . . deuced badly."

He had then paused for a moment to goggle at Humphrey, before going on more quietly: "I do believe you really know nothing of it all as you say . . ."

"No more do I! Not a whit!"

"Pray think, Humph! A fellow nigh as lofty as you are yourself, in dragoon togs, calling us all bosky puppies, then telling everyone in the Tap that you had insulted him!"

"And had I?" the Earl said wonderingly.

"Ay, most assuredly you had! Several times over!

And with a fine flow of language that I never suspicioned you possessed!"

Humphrey had rubbed his throbbing temples, in a futile attempt to bestir matters within them. "It is no use," he muttered thickly. "I still remember naught of this affair."

"*My God . . . !*"

The Earl had then regarded his companion with suddenly narrowed eyes, as he bethought him that Masterson here had an odd turn of humour sometimes. Could it be that he was giving rein to it now? "Dick—you aren't funning me, are you?" he enquired with a flicker of hope. But the other's unwavering glassy stare had been answer enough without the sobering words:

"His 'friend' waited on me only an hour ago, when I was still abed."

"Well, and did you?" Miss Thouvenal demanded in her straighforward style.

"Are you asking me if I cried off from the challenge?"

Humphrey's young mouth had tightened to a line that the young lady had not seen before, but she pushed on blithely: "Not exactly, my lord. I meant did you cut and run as Mr. Masterson was urging you?"

But even she was then made aware of the prickling silence which had invaded their corner of the diligence. Then the Earl informed her, with icy civility, that the course of action she alluded to had not been considered by him as a solution to his predicament.

But his self-control faltered when he came to tell her of the duel itself. The full horror of it was even now still too close to shake himself free from; his

voice trembled repeatedly, adding some additional
dramatic effect to a scene which, in all truth, scarcely
needed it.

"It took place at dawn, in the usual way of such
encounters," he began stiffly.

"Where? At Tunbridge Wells again?"

"Oh no: the Major was stationed close by there.
For that reason alone it would not have done, quite
apart from considerations of . . ."

He paused irritably at having to explain to this
mature-seeming ninnyhammer that the conventions
of fashionable resorts did not usually extend to ac-
commodating affairs of honour. "It was at a village
several miles from there named Stelling Minnis," he
told her shortly. "Situated not far from my home, on
the other side of Canterbury."

"Were you the first one there? Before this major, I
mean?"

"Yes . . . I was."

—And by a good half-hour, in fact. Not only there
first in the physical sense, but there spiritually
quite alone, despite the faithful attendance of Dick
Masterson and Bertram Pollack; both those good old
friends rendered remote and unfamiliar because of
their formal attire in the dim light; standing with
him in an awkward (and distressingly facetious)
little group on the edge of Johnson's Clearing—
where it was said Major Hipsley had already claimed
a fatal victory at an earlier stage in the gaining of
his notorious reputation; and where, right then, a
keen wind coming off the Channel was further chilling
the blood in Humphrey's veins.

"Yes, of course I was in a quake of fright," he
snapped at her in answer to a further question. "If
any man says that he was not, in that situation—
well, hail him for a hero if you choose to, but despise

his hypocrisy if you trust my own opinion of him ...
And I should have been in even worse case had I
been sober," he told her with similar determined
candour.

"What? You were foxed *again!*" she exclaimed.

"Yes, but this time by design rather than accident.
You see ... it is so hard for me to explain now how I
felt then, but I was quite sure in my mind that this
murderous major would kill me, just as he had
snuffed out all those other poor fellows—some of
them slap-up shots, by the bye—whom he'd called
out on some pretext or other."

He glanced at her face, then added impatiently:
"Any man in London would know this, but perhaps I
should explain to you that Hipsley's prowess with
pistols is more than formidable. He has out-pointed
Joe Manton himself on no less than three occasions,
and keeps in regular trim at the gallery of that
name. He uses weapons made to his grip by Manton
himself. Oh, believe me, Miss Thouvenal, I was not
guilty of poetical morbidity in fancying that
Johnson's Clearing would be the very last piece of
England that I would ever see," he concluded with
quiet sincerity.

His words were not without effect. "Pray go on,
sir," said Miss Thouvenal in the most chastened and
serious tone he had yet heard from her.

"Well, at some point in the interminable hours
before the rendezvous it had struck me forcibly that
as drink had been the means of my embroilment in
this affair, then I might as lief have deliberate
recourse to it again in order to make the manner of
my passing more comfortable. I should emphasise
that I did *not* propose taking half so much as had led
me, on that first bout with Hipsley, to miss discern-
ing him altogether!—merely enough to allow me to

present an honourable face to both him and my
friends: and one which would gain me, perhaps, a
dab of credit when the matter afterwards became
public—as I knew it must, with the involvement of
such an adversary as the Major."

"Where had you come by drink at that early
hour?" interposed his practical-minded auditor. "Or
had you a flask in your pocket?"

"No. The three of us knocked up a hedge tavern
near the Minnis, around two in the morning. The
people there let us fetch out a half-barrel on the
patch of grass before the tavern, and between us we
drank it near dry there in the moonlight until it was
time for the rendezvous. I had by far the most drink:
but it accounted in part for a certain forced facetious-
ness on my friends' side, as it accounted wholly for
my own sad work," he said without change of expression. That this tale could hardly put him in
charity with her no longer concerned him, so lost
was he once again in the searing bitterness of his
fate. "And now—if you would kindly not interrupt—I
will try to tell you how that most extraordinary duel
went off, and why I am here to speak of it now."

"Oh, pray do, my lord, for I am truly agog to come
to the kernel of all this roundaboutation! But do not
spin it out too thin, for I know from our last time
over this stretch of ground we now pass that Paris is
close."

"Well then, in brief: Hipsley had with him in his
curricle a brother officer who was his usual second,
and a doctor who also had accompanied the Major on
previous bleak dawns when his weapon had wreaked
professional havoc for the practitioner to either
repair or else certify as beyond it. This doctor was a
very fat fellow and seated bodkin, and our enemy
trio altogether made a deuced tight press in the

curricle. I think that was what made me begin laughing, even before any of them stepped down . . ." Humphrey said gloomily, with his face the same dour cast it had remained in throughout the time while Miss Thouvenal was speaking with him.

"You—laughing?" she cried with incredulity. "And laughing *then?"*

"Ah well, it was the liquor which laughed," he reminded her, with the same dogged honesty he was resolved to preserve until the end of the story. "But I expect that you are familiar with the symptoms of certain states of humour, whether they be induced by intoxication or not: once you are well launched, it is all but impossible to hold back and become serious again."

Miss Thouvenal was now eyeing him in a way that suggested she might be making a reappraisal of his character; not that he cared a rush what she thought or did not think of him. He continued woodenly: "I may say that my two formerly waggish companions were, by this stage, as far from deriving amusement themselves from this meeting as any men could be. For—unlike their sodden principal—they were sober enough to mark Hipsley's hard face, grimacing with fury in the white moonbeams filling the ground: they could also see the silver of the famous duelling pistol, gleaming at his side: they were filled with dread that some move on their own part might turn the lame tiger's wrath on to them, too, once he had devoured me!

"Naturally they now both bent all their efforts not to *raise* my spirits for this moment, as had been their kindly aim before, but on the contrary to speedily *depress* them to a proper awareness of the desperate straits I was in . . ."

Humphrey shook his head in wry resignation.

"But it was not a particle of use. Everything that
now followed on seemed to fit, in my eyes at least, to
a pattern of nonsensical absurdity. I could simply no
longer feel the fear that was still within me. The
laughter which I have spoken of—though it was so
very shocking on such an occasion—seemed to keep
my fear at bay as effectively as the drink had achieved
earlier . . . Oh, I just *cannot tell* of my feelings or
conduct then!" he murmured in despair. "Not, at
least, to—"

"To somebody who has never been foxed in her
life, and never called out by one who had killed nine
others?" said Miss Thouvenal in her crispest grown-up
tones.

"Precisely so!"

"Then try!"

"But I am persuaded I ought not to," he told her,
with maddening primness.

A small foot struck the coach floor again. "Then,
sir, don't try to!" cried his sorely-tried listener. "Just
tell me instead *what happened* out of all this imbro-
glio!"

At which entreaty his face seemed to grow yet
gloomier; if that were possible.

"The second had helped him down—and then at
once had to hold him up. The doctor propped him on
his other side: appearing slightly nonplussed at this
early need of his services. We could discern that the
second was wearing some foot regiment's uniform,
but Hipsley himself was not in his dragoons but a
heavy benjamin with several capes: which made him
more than ever resemble a helpless old man in my
besotted eyes. The moon caught his new splint under
the coat most pathetically, I fancied.

"The second also gripped a guncase, and the doctor
his bag of instruments likewise. As the three came

towards us across the ground, I saw that the Major was fairly gibbering with rage at his enforced reduction to this mode of approach. The infantry officer coughed and said to Dick Masterson: 'Good morning sir. Our weapons, and if I could briefly see yours . . . would twenty-five yards suit you well enough?"

" 'The devil it would, sir,' Dick spoke up gamely—though sounding very hoarse. 'Our man is no shot.' (Just as though I were not there: as indeed I scarcely was. I was still lost in my fatal false mirth.)

" 'Fifteen, then?'

" 'Fifteen yards, old fellow?' Dick referred to me, but even then I could only grin and giggle at Hipsley's contorted features.

"The infantry officer frowned, and stepped closer to look me over. Then he turned aside and spoke quietly to his principal, but Hipsley soon waved him violently away with the first words I had heard him speak, in a voice which was surprisingly deep-pitched and musical: 'I care not a (you can imagine his precise words, Miss Thouvenal) for that! The pup was bosky before when he worsted me, so let us see if he can o'erturn those same odds again!'

"The second murmured to him once more, but this time he scarcely listened before bellowing: 'I'd as soon have been *reconciled* to an engagement at Tyburn Tree than postpone this one here for another second, damn you, Stephen! *Get on with it!*'

"The foot officer half-shrugged to us in embarrassment, then walked off to pace out the ground. Presently he and the medical attendant aided their implacable principal to take up his position at the place agreed."

The Earl now passed a hand across his brow, and the young lady saw that it shook.

"Bertie Pollack had made himself responsible for

my weapons. They were hired: since we country boys were used to firing naught but sporting guns for pigeon and the like . . . I swear I had never touched a pistol in my life before that morning," he declared in a kind of dulled desperation.

Miss Thouvenal misunderstood that quiver in his voice. She merely said, impressed: "So indeed it should have turned out cold-blooded murder!" She was eying him now with a certain stupid respect which galled him far more than her usual pertness.

"Indeed it almost did," he told her savagely. "Though not as you suppose . . . It was agreed that we were to fire upon the drop of the foot officer's handkerchief. The latter gentleman had impressed that upon me several times, to ensure that I understood it even in stupor. Major Hipsley—after some difficulty—removed his coat, shook off his doctor as the handkerchief was raised, and stood unassisted for the crucial moment: turning sidewise towards me in the very picture of the skilled duellist. And then—" His lordship was suddenly short of the words to continue with.

"*Yes, then?*" squeaked Miss Thouvenal, in a veritable agony of suspense.

Humphrey abandoned the futile, last-second temptation to dress up his shame in some way. "Then I raised the pistol," he grated loudly, so that half the coach could hear if not understand him. "I had some cawkerish notion in my skull that I must fix it upon cock—not realising that all such preliminaries had been looked to for me by Dick Masterson. You must remember," he said intensely, "that I was still very drunk, still very amused (God forgive me) by all that I am relating to you."

Miss Thouvenal was now too wrought up in the story even to chide him any more. She sat in tense silence on the very edge of her jolting seat (for they were now passing over Parisian cobbles) and waited for the distraught young nobleman to conclude in his own way.

He did so with jerky succinctness that stemmed clearly from deepest revulsion.

". . . I learned only later that I had taken hold of the weapon upside-down . . . I must have moved the trigger itself rather than merely the hammer as I had intended . . . the shock of the concussion, the sudden stench of powder . . . roused me to cold sobriety long before the echo had died away into the black trees around the Clearing . . . Hipsley fell, with the handkerchief still held up clearly and damningly at full arm-stretch by the frozen figure of the other officer . . . and Dick Masterson shouted to me, in a voice of contempt and near-hatred that shrivelled my soul: *'Are you run mad, Humph? Do you know what you have done?—you have shot him down like a dog!'* "

"But not killed him, at least?" Miss Thouvenal ventured, after a full half-minute of wide-eyed restraint on her part.

He gave her a smile that barely altered the line of his mouth. "I dare swear it would have been vastly better for both of us if I had killed him! For consider: he had now irrevocably lost his vaunted reputation, whate'er else he had saved—which, to that sort of a fellow, is a form of living death, I'm persuaded. Whilst I on my side had gained a very opposite one—literally in a flash—which I must bear until the day I am no more!" he declared ringingly.

But this youthful dramatics was doing it much too brown for a practical-minded female to appreciate. "But surely, if the Major was no more than wounded—?"

"Wounded you say! Aye, but consider the malignant manner of that wounding! I have thought back on it all so often that I can view it now just as it must have seemed to him then: lying with his face in the mud of Johnson's Clearing, and knowing that *his other leg was broken, and by me of all men*! And broken, moreover, in the most despicable, dishonourable manner that anyone could ever conceive!"

Anne Thouvenal let out a long breath as she comprehended the full import of her travelling companion's astonishing survival as a duellist.

Having no brothers, only sisters, and a father who was dead, as yet she was personally unfamiliar with the scruples and niceties of masculine comportment. But, despite her forthright manner, she was still very much a child of her time. It occurred to her now that there was truly something reprehensible in this young man's admitted behaviour. Perhaps he had been singularly ill-starred, as it indeed appeared; but the blunt fact remained that his conduct had plainly not been quite the thing.

It was but a short step from this critical reflection to the young lady's following thought: that her Mama had been most typically lax and remiss in allowing a stranger to converse with her in this public coach. However, it was a lapse that was about to correct itself, judging by the postillion's urgent cries and the squealing sound of brakes.

She rose haughtily to her feet after the coach's final lurch. In her most precocious adult manner she told Humphrey: "It has been most . . . interesting conversing with you, my lord. Allow me to wish you well on the Tour. I hope that it may improve you," she said with emphasis, making her way through the press of now upright passengers towards her family.

Humphrey nodded bitterly, both at Miss Thouvenal's stiff back and to himself; for he had anticipated her response precisely. In fact, this parting coldness rather raised than lowered her in his estimation, that she should have responded with propriety to his sordid revelations. Evidently she was more genteel than first appearance had suggested.

Shaking Mr Mayhew awake from his slumbers with rather undue harshness, Humphrey too made ready to leave the diligence and commence his exile proper.

Three

The leaves in the park were tinted yellow by the time that Samuel Mayhew's first lengthy letter reached his patron.

The Most Honourable the Marquis of Cornford studied the missive in the Little Drawing-room at Hoadoak, which had become his own private room after the death of his lady five years previously.

He was a large and solid man with none of his son's lean tallness, and with little of the country dweller about his appearance despite the fact that he had now been confined to Hoadoak and its demesnelands for several years. The intermittent, but historical tendency of male members of the Freen family towards a form of paralytick affliction of the lower limbs when past maturity had seemed to spare him until his sixty-fifth year; but then it had gripped him tight-fast, as he sometimes averted to it. But he could still walk without the arm of a footman, and still dress himself with only slight assistance in the style that had been fashionable when he was a younger man: which was, in coats that were almost devoid of cutaway line, and with neckcloths whose elegance was a living reproach to the starched fribbling which he deplored (amongst much else besides) in his son's contemporaries.

Not that Humphrey himself caused him any vexation on that head; at least, with all his faults, he was as plain and down-to-earth a fellow as his father could have wished for in his only son. Indeed, until the untoward and shameful tangle with Major Hipsley, the hope of his House had showed every sign of possessing uncommon good sense. Made morose by that reflection, he now picked up the thread again in the Chaplain's letter.

'. . . and so finally we left Paris and embarked upon the *coche d'eau*—as they term their crude river boats. I cannot speak for Lord Begbroke, since he appeared taken with the place, but for my own part I was well pleased to see the back of it! What eloquent words did Walpole employ to describe it?— something, I collect, along the lines of a dirty town with a dirtier ditch running through called the Seine—truly I can echo and endorse that sentiment with all my soul! And Rousseau's opinion also seems not only quite *natural*, as one would expect, but also eminently sagacious: All the time I was there I was but scheming how I should depart. Now, as you well know, my lord, I am no more an admirer of that wild fellow than I care for the Perpetrator of Gothick Taste, but for the life of me I cannot dispute either of their dispassionate verdicts on this odious capital! And furthermore, *never* have I consumed such high-seasoned cookery, w'ch you have my personal assurance is quite as bad as most travellers say . . .'

With a bored sigh, the Marquis lifted his eyes from the pages with their violent under-scoring and gazed out of the window near his table. He looked across the lawn to where sheep grazed on unscythed grass, beyond the faintly discernible line of a ha-ha, their white forms distinct against the final easterly slopes of the North Downs. His still meaty, slightly dissipated face was sardonic and brooding as he continued to finger the letter. Not much had made him actually laugh of recent years, but he was amused a little now to think of his worthy Chaplain responding so predictably to Paris.

Paris . . . He smiled less crookedly, and fetched his eyes inside again to look up at a picture hanging in the room. It was Nicolle's *La Seine du Louvre,* and it had been purchased at the time when he himself had made the Tour as a young man. It could still convey to him, even now in ill-health and old age, what the personal discovery of Paris had once meant to him.

Of course he knew it was idle to suppose that his stolid Humphrey could have responded to the great city in any like fashion. Even less than the Reverend Mayhew was *he* likely to appreciate its various un-English charms. Indeed, had he packed the boy abroad for any more subtle purpose than to safeguard his life from further assaults upon it by the justly enraged officer of Dragoons, he would assuredly have contrived in vain . . .

Once more he returned to the letter, re-reading some lines and then passing on to more of Mr Mayhew's reproaches to him that were couched in the guise of information. Hurrying through a whole mass of such cowardly complaint he came to:

'. . . whereupon we decided against diverting to Notorious Marseilles, being sufficiently well pleased with Aix and Arles.'

Once again the contemptuous reference to ancient French places brought a bright flash of memory into the Marquis's pale blue, red-rimmed eyes. Now he

was remembering stepping down to the harbour at
Marseilles, to see Louis' galleys. He had actually
conversed with a slave there, had inspected the weals
on his back, and had afterwards recorded an interesting conversation with him in his Continental
Diary. But, of course, to the likes of young Humph
and Sam Mayhew, such a place was merely 'Notorious
Marseilles'. Thomas Freen crinkled his face in dis-
gust at such complacent parochialism, and wondered
whether, as his heir's plodding progress about Europe
continued, the punitive effects of exile might not be
surpassed by his own pain in reading of them.

Perhaps with that apprehension in mind, he had
adjured his Chaplain not to trouble himself to write
home very often; and it was the following springtime
before another missive from his hand came to
Hoadoak; this time bearing a Swiss postmark.

That letter, however, was not so much peevish in
tone as highly excitable: for the writer had just
learned of Bonaparte's escape from Elba, and his
swift march on Paris. The letter was full of entreaties for guidance and instruction; it spoke wildly of
thoughts of the two Tourists 'fleeing Home straightway across the Alps', if this course of action was
sanctioned by the writer's noble patron. Repressing
his amusement (at least on paper) the Marquis replied urging both calm and due caution on them.
They were to ignore Boney's probably brief recovery
and stay safely amongst the Swiss until he directed
them to proceed to Italy—which, in fact, he did as
soon as the period of the Hundred Days terminated
at Waterloo.

Then there followed a differently plaintive letter
from the reverend gentleman, composed not long
after the pair had crossed the Alps by way of the
Simplon route. Cornford had finally laughed out

loud in the Little Drawing-room when he read of Mayhew's terrified agonies, against a visual background of his own memories of that huge and awesome terrain. It was clear that the tiresome and temporal-minded cleric had been given a most uncomfortable sense of Eternity whilst he was among the great mountains.

In due course another letter came from Italy which contained an odd reference to '. . . the Earl's character having undergone a distinct and in some ways perturbing change as the Foreign Impressions of his Journeys continue.' But he paid that little heed, concluding merely that even his son must not be quite as impervious to civilizing influence as he had thought him.

He learned in the next autumn the interesting intelligence that Mayhew disliked the German beer; and by that winter the pair were sampling the culture of the Low Countries.

But the Chaplain's second communication from Brussels, despatched the following February, received a more prompt reply than usual, and in a hand which he at first failed to recognise as that of his lordship's agent-in-chief. By the same delivery came some pages for the Earl from his sisters. The former missive bluntly told Mayhew that his patron was very ill; he and his ward were straightway to take the packet for home.

Rawton, Lord Cornford's groom, as he crossed the yard from the stables, was the first to spy the yellow bounder as its four horses clattered past the entrance lodge.

A chamber-maid was just then shaking the end of her mop from an upper window of the house. Rawton promptly stuck two fingers into his mouth and emitted a piercing whistle to draw her attention; then gestured towards the approaching chaise. The maid nodded in understanding and vanished from sight. Reassured that everything proper would now be attended to indoors, the old groom hastened to be the first to welcome the Earl back to his home.

The nature of his journey was confirmed by the lather upon the animals, and by their plumes of heavy breath as they were halted by the entrance. The young postboy on the nearside animal winked wryly at the groom as he came down from the slippery flanks and moved to the door of the equipage, still gripping his whip. But Rawton was there before him. He pulled down the steps and opened the door, seeing first the plump figure of Mr Mayhew and then the vague shape of the Earl on the other side of the carriage.

The groom's lined square face was fixed in a sombre cast which owed only partially to his sense of fitness; for he had been in Lord Cornford's service for a long time, and felt his sudden failing keenly as he waited now to greet his son.

But that expression changed to one of pure astonishment as the travellers began to descend stiffly. For although the Reverend appeared just as he remembered him from two years back, the Earl himself . . .

He had last seen young Humphrey in a coat of torn brown drab, and in knee breeches whose style had always put him in mind of his own grandfather's. That was how he had been rigged the day when he, Rawton, had taken him and the Chaplain in the dogcart to Canterbury, there to board the Dover Mail.

Now he found himself gaping at the self-same lofty figure—but resplendent in a striking hat, in dazzling white pantaloons, and in foreign-looking Hessians with sharp toes and white tops—and decorated with long greenish fringes! While as for his neckcloth—well, Joby Rawton was no connoisseur of young bucks' neckcloths, but he *did* know that the intricacies of the creation which was now before his eyes bore about as much resemblance to the mode. Humphrey had used to favour as a brilliant India peacock resembled a farmyard fowl. His unnerved gaze shied off it to where numerous glittering fobs and seals hung from the Earl's waistband. At last he looked at his face; and that (not merely because it seemed thinner) was somehow the biggest change of all.

"Stand back, gapeseed!" snapped the Chaplain with all his old familiar rasp. "What news of your master?"

"He is much the same, sir, I think." Joby was still staring in fascination as the Earl's boot-fringes slapped against the footboard as he stepped down.

"You *think*? What is that supposed to signify?" demanded Mr Mayhew. Once again he had travelled badly across the Channel and his temper showed it. "Speak out—stretch your mind to try to apprehend that the little we have been told was hardly enough to ease my own concern—let alone to allay the protracted natural anxieties of his lordship here."

Joby Rawton here grinned a little to himself, as he caught the new creamy manner towards Humphrey which Mayhew had now dropped into. Formerly, he had been used to roasting the lad almost as if he were a servant like himself. That was one change, however, that failed to surprise the groom in the least as things stood; since he had long opined that the Reverend was a deep old file under all the flummery. He told him: "Sir, I only know that both the sawbones who are in attendance have been closeted with him since two nights ago."

"Yes, yes, but the *nature of the ailment*?—or else must I ask the steward for a sensible answer?—as I see he is at last come to meet us!"

Rawton hesitated, reluctant to repeat the perhaps ignorant kitchen talk he was privy to, but misliking just as much to have the top-lofty steward steal his thunder. "They do say that neither of the doctors knows what it is," he volunteered finally.

"And that don't vastly astonish me, Sam," said Humphrey, speaking at last. (And in a languid, drawling manner that seemed as peculiar to the groom as the rest of him.) "I dare swear that both these gentlemen—one of them is his usual Suddaby, no doubt—have been franked more handsomely for their two nights' work than he saw fit to extend to us during these as many years: but I collect I can run down this case as well as any leech. Why look further, Samuel, as I said to you on the boat, than for some intensifying of the well-known family weakness, what else?" He pulled off one immaculate white glove as he pronounced that lay theory; revealing yet another collection of shining metal about most of his fingers, and raising his hand to admire the rings in the afternoon sunlight.

"You're out there," Rawton told him with a bluntness he could not restrain. He found it shocking that the Earl was still dawdling outside with the likes of himself, and not racing up the stairway to be with my lord. "Whate'er else, his stiffness ain't done it to him, for Mr. Suddaby said so to Jim Harrow, without a shred of doubt!"

"Hand-downs from that jobbernoll Harrow!" Mayhew scoffed ". . . Ah, how-de-doo, Steward, we are glad to see you *finally* . . . Oh yes, my lord, I am persuaded that you are entirely in the right of it: why indeed should we look any further for the cause when, alas, so many of your noble forebears . . ." He paused with delicacy before continuing: "I am only too conscious that no words of mine, in these most arduous last moments of your impatience to be with him, can hope to lighten your burden to any degree: but I venture to say that it is truly a solace to me to know that your lordship shows no sign whatever of that taint, no remotest indication of—"

"Sam, leave me now," the Earl interjected loudly. "We have been together for these past two years, almost continually. That, I do believe, is sufficient for the moment."

"Of course, of course, you wish to proceed straightway to his chamber . . . so natural—and so thoughtless of me," the fawning cleric responded, his complexion now tinged with pink.

"Devil a bit—I want to wash!"

And with that set-down, those unfilial words, and a curt nod to the steward, Humphrey stepped up to the portico and passed inside down the avenue of assembled servants, followed at a cautious distance by his humiliated late bear-leader.

Joby Rawton, who still stood beside the post-chaise, had now coloured up a little himself. For he and the Earl had always used to be like winking together, yet he had ignored his honest words of welcome without even the barest civility.

The old groom tried to tell himself that the melancholy of the occasion accounted for the Earl's odd behaviour. He could see that might be the reason, though he was far from convinced. And, most assuredly, it could not account for the young man's outlandish clothes. Puzzled and hurt, his eyes met those of the senior postboy on the box who by now

had unloaded the travellers' luggage and was about
to clasp the reins again. Rawton said to him: "Hey,
d'you lads fancy a mug of wet before you wheel
about? After me, then."

A little while later Rawton was the centre of
considerable interest and attention in the Room.

"His young lordship was like that to *you*, who
taught him to ride when he was in short coats!"
exclaimed Mrs Boon, the housekeeper. "I must say it
don't sound the leastest bit like him, not as I remember him."

"I tell you, he's come back different," Rawton said
dourly for the third time. "He's rigged out in such
style as you never saw—a regular Tulip, or whatever
they calls 'em. Don't ask my why or how, but it's a
fact. And it's not just that he's niffy-naffy in his
ways like he never was before, but he hardly speaks
now, and when he does his tongue's dipped in vine-
gar. My, but you should have heard how he roasted
the Rev'rend!" he broke off, grinning at that particular example of the Earl's altered disposition.

"That one's not changed, I'll wagerr," said the
groom of chambers, who was a dour Scot in his
mid-fifties.

"—And you'd lose your rhino, Jock," the old groom
replied more dourly still. "Oh, he's caught the tide
going out, never you fret . . . Now young Hump is
become 'his lordship this' and 'his lordship that' with
the old lickpenny! And when you think how rough-
shod he was used to ride that boy, I dunno . . . Not
that Humphrey don't see through him, for he makes
it plain enough he does."

"If you ask me, it's my lord's riding so rusty on the
lad what's the bottom of it," opined Mr Leach; who
had been the cook for many years at the house in
Mount Street and now, for as many more, here in the

country. He was a taciturn man with a knowing air which did not always endear him to the rest of the Room.

"Still, maybe Humphrey and old mealy-mouth being together like, amongst the Froggies and such, for all of two years, has made them deal pretty arm-in-armly together most times," put in Lord Cornford's under-employed valet. "Humphrey will come about soon enough now he's home again, you'll see . . ."

And as that upper servant was far above the old groom's touch, Joby Rawton merely grunted sceptically back at him and then whispered in the house-keeper's ready ear: "I don't care a jot what Percy Manning thinks! That boy's come back to us half flash and half foolish, and up to his neck in bile besides! This place is in for rare kick-ups *when the time comes,* and you mark I said so . . . Now, d'you reckon Leachy has another slice of cold meat tucked away somewhere for me, Mrs B? Ask him for me, there's my sweetheart—for you know how to whee-dle round him, and I just ain't got the knack nor the inclination neither!"

The Earl had now finished before his shaving-stand and, under Manning's bemused stare, was presently engaged in fashioning a fresh necktie of the same convoluted style which had so shaken the old groom upon his arrival.

Now it was Percy Manning who could not take his eyes off that intricate and highly-wrought fantasy in linen, as he speechlessly observed the toil of its formation in the pierglass; for the valet, like his former young master, was country-bred and ac-customed to plain modes of fashion.

Conscious of this scrutiny, Humphrey endeavoured

to coax the snowy folds into place, but his face was growing red against the cloth. He was now ruefully learning, as many a young gentleman had learned before him, that the Oriental was imbued with certain treacherous qualities which required a long apprenticeship before the casual mastery, which he now attempted to demonstrate before his servant, could always be successful.

Manning watched his repeated tries with mounting professional vexation. Finally, goaded beyond his normal deference, and sensible that, after all, he knew this arrogant stranger from boyhood, he blurted out: "Oh, my God, sir—let me, pray!—now, let's see—it's a rare piece of bobbery, ain't it, but *this* must surely first go *there*, see? And then we gets to proceeding with the twirly-whirlying—like so. Now, you build on that," he said tactfully, stepping away from the glass and not much caring for the Earl's glowering crestfallen features as he saw them reflected in it.

But all that was said to him in reply, with the same untoward new stiffness, was: "I am obliged, Percy. And now the pantaloons, if you have them there."

"Oh, *them*, yes, but—since you'll be going in to your father and also ... what with them being a mite travel-grimed, I thought—but I'll fetch 'em directly," the valet stuttered, making in haste for the door.

"I thank you: and do you also bring back those Italian boots of mine you so disapprove."

Percy hovered unhappily in the doorway. "It ain't that *I* disapprove, sir, it's only that I'm persuaded your poor f—"

"Just so—the boots too, if you please."

And those cold, different eyes now moved back to

the looking-glass as he made final passes to the tie; which, by this stage, had his shirt-points jaggedly encircling his neck in the approved style, which permitted only the slightest movement to either side without exacting acute punishment.

When his man had returned and his dressing was completed, he told him calmly: "Go now to that brace of quacks with my father and present my compliments and tell them I want them out of there in five minutes' time, when I shall go to him. I shall remain with him for a further five minutes precisely, until six o'clock. Then I shall dine with my sisters—nay, I mean with Lady Philippa only. And you can tell them downstairs we won't require Chenson—one footman will do."

But that iron composure he had brought home with him faltered when he opened the door into the familiar wainscoted room, still hung with faded blue damask from his mother's time, and regarded the figure lying on the bed.

He approached it woodenly, saying in a forced and husky tone: "Well then, I am returned as you bade me. Do you know what ails you? I collect the leeches don't."

The grey head rolled slowly on the pillow, and the Marquis blinked several times in an effort to focus upon his heir—a process of recognition made hard enough by the curious mist which was now often in front of him; and the more so by the total stranger whom he finally managed to see.

He cleared his throat with similar laboured difficulty, then uttered, with a firm distinctness that would have astonished his two physicians: "You left here a knave . . . and I see you are come back a coxcomb . . ."

"Oh, pleasant address indeed!" the Earl burst forth

savagely, turning aside from his attentive stoop over
the sick-bed and striding up and down the chamber
on his long legs. "And *I* see, for my part, that the
years you have been spared my disgracing presence
have sweetened you famously! Why pull me back to
you, then, like a figure in a raree show, when I was
at last enjoying the Tour?—or was that your design
too, eh? Did you apprehend the dire chance that I
might actually be experiencing *happiness*, and stage
a *female spasm* in order to curtail it, my dear father?
I own I should not be surprised! But if that was your
scheme I must disappoint you by saying it did not
quite answer! Since, once I learned that the banishment was over, I went out and spent *nigh every last
groat* of the miserly few you spared us—to buy these
fashionable continental clothes! And that made me
vastly happy!"

He continued in the same stormy, reckless manner: "For I had grown very tired of my false indi-
gence, which stemmed from no necessity of depriva-
tion—all Kent knows you are the richest man in
it!—but solely from your cruel desire to punish me at
a time when I had merited *nothing but your natural
sympathy*! And I had also grown tired of climbing
grotesque mountains, with that whining fat gaby
you had set upon my back! But by the time I was
amongst the Italians and the Hollanders, I *did* finally enjoy the Tour—as you certainly never believed
I was capable or else you would not have sent me!
And I perceive myself that it has changed me, as it
has changed others likewise. And I hope you may
learn to like the change, for you contrived it *and
now, by God, you can acquire the habit of franking it*!
And I promise you—from this day I intend to live *en
prince!*"

At last, even this tumult of blind rage abated as

he drew breath; and with pause came recollection of present circumstances rather than past ones; and a sudden cold knowledge that the pathetic figure in the bed was no callous shammer, but his very ill parent. Then the onset of shame and remorse was swift and overwhelming. Becoming momently more distressed by what he had said, he turned and blindly left the chamber.

Four

When he had first encountered his eldest sister, upon entering the hall from the post-chaise, Lady Philippa had been redolent of eau-de-Cologne compounded with sal volatile; and was in the act of sniffing some other portable restorative from a crystal phial she held in her hand. She had tottered forward to him like an old woman, uttering a low cry and holding out her tearful face to his; as the assembled servants watched the moving scene with deep appreciation.

"... Oh *Humph*, Humphy *dear*, you are come home at last—and at *such a time!*" she had wailed in his ear-drum.

"Pip—please—not now!" he had begged her in a whisper, feeling fagged to death from the journey and the whole situation he had returned to.

"—And so elegant!" she exclaimed next, releasing him and standing back to take in the full strange effect with her widening wet eyes. "I hardly know you, Humphy!"

"Lord help me, then, if that were not true!" he grunted, skirmishing his way with care around

Philippa (who was wearing what appeared to be a style of anticipatory mourning) and kissing the other two girls with affection but determined formality. Then he had passed on without further ado towards the great stair.

But now, his elder sister was more composed than he was. They dined together at a corner of the long table, lighted only by a single candle-branch above them on the wall; in deference to their absent parent's nip-cheese ways in all matters of holding household. Buy by this time Philippa had realised that it was more of a priority to cheer her brother than to defer to the sick man upstairs; and she had chosen an evening dress in the latest gay fashion of two colours—blue bodice and pink skirt, with a fine sapphire necklace and bracelet. Also she had seen to it that this homecoming was celebrated, if not with the joyfulness that would have pertained at any other time, at least by Humphrey's eating his first meal off the Crown Derby with the Chantilly pattern; which, she felt vaguely, was suited to a returned Tourist.

But if her strange new exquisite of a brother was at all conscious of the French sprigs which showed here and there around his gravy, he gave little sign of it as he picked his way moodily through boiled leg of lamb, roast chicken, and even the fragile pancakes which were Leach's pride.

"Humphy, you're not eating a thing!" she reproached him fondly.

"No—the consequence of over-much Holland stodginess, I expect, and then the usual cavalier treatment from that dev'lish strip of ocean!" he replied with a dull attempt at lightness.

Lady Philippa was tall like her brother; as still showed when both were seated as now. 'We Freens cannot sit—we crouch like beasts,' Humphrey had once joked her in happier days. Although in fact Ellen and Margaret, his other twin sisters, were short-ish girls, as Philippa was ruefully aware. They were the youngest of the family; she herself preceding Humphrey by one year.

Realising that she was nonplussed with him, he made an effort to shake off the dismal mood which had been with him ever since coming downstairs from his father. He said in an altered tone: "By the bye, when I was in Rome I exchanged bows with our cousin Edgehill, did father tell you?"

She creased her blonde brows which were another feature they shared. "I don't remember . . . perhaps he did," she amended hastily, still conscious of the paramount need to peace-make between the men of her family. "That would be some time ago now, wouldn't it? Since what has happened I find I cannot put my mind to—buy why only a bow, pray?" She caught herself up again and smiled brightly. "If you mean John Edgehill, I must say that was unkind in you. Why, I collect that you and he were always close."

"Aye, it was John," he grunted, toying now with his wine glass. "And a regular Jack-pudding he made of himself, there amongst the temples of antiquity."

She looked at him in bewilderment. For when she had described him as close with their cousin, she knew that she had much understated the case. In fact they had been at Harrow together, and had roamed most of the Home Counties, as thick as bees, during and after their schooldays. Thoughtfully eyeing his tall neck-cloth and other splendours afresh, she murmured: "You found John—a trifle out of style in that setting?"

"Not precisely: I found *myself* out of style, and saw how—through the amiable John—I too must have appeared to the Roman citizens—who, I must tell you, Pip, are the most cultivated race on Earth! To be one of their society, tho' only for the short time the Tour allowed, was an experience like ... oh, I can't express! Like coming in from dark to light, truly! I liked the Hollanders also, well enough, afterwards—for I saw them with eyes which were then opened to all of Europe. But if my *dear father* had only sported enough blunt for us to be well to pass whilst in Italy, instead of keeping us like church mice, I would have undertaken to stay there away from him, in perfect bliss, for as long as he could ever have wished for!"

Bitterness had crept back into his tone despite the warmth and fervour of his recollections. Philippa said defensively: "I am quite poz he did not mean to—"

"Oh yes he did! If you had been a fly on the wall just now when I was with him, you would have very little doubt in your mind as to his enduring opinion of me—whatever I am like!"

"Humphy, dear, he *is* very ill ..." she remonstrated gently.

They were both silent as the footman came and removed the first cloth and served dessert. Then Humphrey told her: "Of course I know he is ill—do you think me a nodcock? That consideration was first in my mind before I went to him, yet when he gave me snuff once more, after such a long absence ... well, I fear I rendered him Turkish treatment in kind, despite every good intention."

"Oh *no*!" With a hand to her mouth she had half-risen from the table in daughterly agitation. "Did you ... overset him?"

He uttered a harsh bark of laughter. "Do not distress yourself on that head, at least! For coming to cuffs with me has never in the least degree overset him! It lies outside *my* power to command a natural response from him! You should know that as well as anyone—you were at home here, were you not, when all the farradiddle of my banishment was being arranged? I misremember now, but I fancy you were . . . I do not deny that this evening I paid off my debt of rancour to him in full—tho' I am ashamed to say so. But be assured that all *he* did was *doze*—howsoever I ripped up at him!"

Lady Philippa re-seated herself with a sigh of relief. "I collect he was merely tired . . . Humphy, you must not repine at anything he may have said to you, or that you said when goaded: for I, too, have had to bear much uncharacteristic spleen from him these past weeks."

"Uncharacteristic?" he said witheringly, biting on an apple. "Hah!"

"We should both try to think of him as he was used to be, before you—" She bit her lip, then continued with resolution: "Before you duelled with the cavalry officer, he was always an affectionate and generous father, as you must own if you are fair to him."

He gave a grudging nod; though at once amending that agreement with: "In his manner towards you, Pip, maybe. He was always indulgent to females, whether those of his own distaff or . . . but mum for that now."

Apprehending that they had fallen into a way of speech which would have been more fitting if their parent was no more, he changed the subject abruptly. "And what have you been about these past years while I was away? Breaking more hearts? You must

have come out, I collect. Did father stand the nonsense for that much at least?"

This tender brotherly enquiry elicited a somewhat
wintry smile from Lady Philippa. "I was presented
two seasons ago, to be precise, with a considerable
expenditure," she told him; a distinct warning edge
to her voice that his ear had now grown deaf to.

"And did you take well, eh? Am I soon to acquire
some honest sprig of London fashion as my brother-
in-law?" Smiling condescendingly at that thought,
he admired his foreign rings under the candles; then
fell to toying with what she privately regarded as
his rather shocking Roman quizzing-glass.

"You are not," she said dryly, repressing her irritation. "Almost—at one time—at least, I thought—
but no."

In fact, there had been not merely one but three
occasions since her come-out when offers had been
made her. The first two had been confidently rejected
by her father. By the time of the third (when a
deepening sense of realism was persuading the Marquis to lower his high expectations), alas, her feelings had not been engaged. She had tried, so very
hard, to love Lord Henry Vaile; to no avail, as she
had ruefully punned to herself when the pain of the
affair was behind her. Lord Henry had been thirty-
five, darkly handsome, eligible enough, of adequate
fortune, altogether a copperplate match for her whom
all her friends had thought her mad for refusing.
She almost thought so too, in retrospect; though still
knowing full well that if the whole ordeal were to be
undergone a second time, there could be no other
outcome without perpetrating a monstrous decep-
tion upon that kind suitor.

Humphrey now broke in, with rather unfeeling
impatience, upon this sad reverie he had set off in

her. "Come, come, there is time enough yet to come about!"

She shoot her fair braids, making a slight grimace. "I think not: I dread the springtime now, if you must know! And this year I must take the twins to town with me—and feel older still! Oh, it is all well enough when one is new to it, and at St James's, and with the Regent saying nice things to one, but—"

"Did he, by ginger! Surely that made a famous beginning?"

She smiled at him tolerantly, with a worldliness that far exceeded his own new affectations, saying: "Humphy—the Regent is known for his beautiful manners to each year's crop of girls. But he also has a habit of delivering amusing little animadversions to his set behind their backs, *which are repeated . . .*"

"Aha, I see!—and in your own case he said—?"

She reddened. "It appears that he said it would make an intolerable stretch to—to stand up with a filly who herself stood twenty hands."

He roared before he could stop himself, then said hastily: "Poor Pippy, what a shame! And doubtless that brilliant utterance became an *on-dit* which cast a blight at Almack's and wherever else you went from that day hence?"

"Our aunt never obtained vouchers for Almack's," she said coolly, rising from the table. "And now, if you really have no wish for any port—and I can see for myself you are plainly bent on eating nothing, despite Leach's best efforts—shall we sit and prose for a while with Ellen and Margaret? The Blue Saloon has been changed since you saw it last and is blue no longer! I know the twins are longing to speak with you."

The Tourist was soon responding good-naturedly

over the tea tray to the several questions which the
twins showered upon him; aware that his arrival
was a timely relief for all his sisters from the burden
of living with the sick man upstairs.

"Humph, do all the ton in Italy wear boots like
yours?" Or: "Humphy, I *cannot* like those brazen
small figures all round your quizzer!" Or: "Humph,
it is hard to believe that it is you in that Bird's Eye
Wipe!"

"Don't be a goosecap, Nell!" ejaculated the other of
the pair, Lady Margaret. "Surely you know by now
that only the Corinthians wear Bird's Eye neckcloths! *That* is most certainly nothing of the kind:
and our brother—despite all the bronze we see in
him from the Tour—is still, I would hazard, no
Corinthian," the young miss said shrewdly.

"Indeed I am not, Meg," he smiled at her. "I have
as little store of patience with the Curricle Crashers
as I had before our father ever packed me—as before
I left England," he amended stiffly. "The moonling
set would never be tolerated in Italy."

"Humphy, do the Paris women paint not only
their faces but the *shoulders too*?" Lady Ellen ran on
with irrepressible eagerness. He looked at her criti-
cally for the first time since his return. She was
another fair one, like Philippa and himself; Margaret
being the sole legatee of their Mama's dark looks,
which now looked down upon her children from a
faded kit-kat over the hearth. But both twins were
grown plumpish during his absence, unlike their
elders. *Female puppyfat,* he reflected learnedly. He
had seen that too in Italy; and sometimes distressingly
prolonged into later life.

"Oh, every one of them! With the same purpose as
the Indian chiefs'," he answered Nell, with a stray
gleam of mischief entering his travel-weary eyes.

"Indian chiefs? Oh Humph, you're gammoning me *already*!" Lady Ellen pouted in vexation. Humphrey noticed that her hair had the appearance of being fresh from curl-papers; and those curls over the ears made her face seem over-broad where nature had already been a trifle too generous with width. And he saw that she still had the awkward trick of pleating her muslin gowns across her knees when excitable. With the same sharpened eyes which greater sophistication (and lack of familiarity) had given him, he also observed that whilst still no beauty, this younger sister was far from being an antidote. And as for Margaret, she seemed to have gained true countenance while he was away.

Philippa now looked up from the piece of embroidery she had on her tambour-frame. "I doubt that he is hoaxing you, Nelly—think, prattlebox!—what qualities might they share, Indian chiefs and Frenchwomen?" she asked Nell in the tone of preceptress which came naturally to her as the eldest.

"Lord, *I* don't know!"

"Why, they both have recourse to daubing so as to terrify their enemies," Humphrey told her, rising and stretching. "Well, I have enjoyed my homecoming in the main, but now I'm more than ready for bed . . . delightful though it has been to see you all again. Yes—I find I'm glad to be home."

But when he had kissed them, more affectionately than when he first arrived, and trudged upstairs to his bedchamber, there was a further period of delay before he could cap his candle. For even as the valet began moving about him there came a discreet knock on the door.

"Yes, what now?" he called irritably, signalling to Percy Manning to be ready to deny him.

"My lord, I know that it is late and you must be

exhausted from your journey, but if I might have a few moments with you before you retire I should rest easier myself. My name is Knight, Stephen Knight."

Sighing, Humphrey bade Manning open the door. The courteous tones came from someone he could not place amongst all the other old faces he had recognised in the last few hours. Standing in the upper hallway was a small grey-haired personage who had a round and rather exhausted face himself, above an archaic military-style stock.

"Ah, you must be the doctor who has been assisting Suddaby . . . how do you do, sir. Percy, you at least can get off to bed, I will attend to myself now . . . Do you step this way, Doctor."

The latter did so, wiping his button nose on a handkerchief of fine lawn. Humphrey montioned him to a chair and re-seated himself, saying, when once the valet had left them: "I trust our people have made you and your servant comfortable? I believe you and Suddaby have been in constant attendance upon my parent for a lengthy time now. I commiserate you," he added dryly, turning on the dressing-stool to unpin his neckcloth, and placing the amethyst pin carefully upon the table.

"Most comfortable, my lord. As to your father— yes, the case has proved stubborn, I regret to say."

Growing slightly impatient with this flat civility, Humphrey now informed his visitor: "I have already heard some stewards' room slum that neither one of you knows what has smitten him." He studied the effect of his words in the mirror.

The London specialist gave a light little laugh of professional scorn for such lay opinion; which, nevertheless, did not convince Humphrey that the rumours he had mentioned were entirely without foundation.

And neither did his next words. "With regard to his *palsystroke*, my lord, alas there can be no conjecture at all on that head."

"A palsy you say? And would that really be unrelated to his former inherited stiffness? And what else, of a speculative nature, have you and old Suddaby discovered, eh?"

The society doctor paused a few seconds to form a judicious reply. He was a shade perplexed by the Earl; who, in his austere middle-aged judgement, looked like a foreign demi-beau; but who also seemed incongruously possessed of a down-to-earth and incisive mind. He had found much the same contrary nature in the younger Prince of Wales, whom he had twice attended professionally at that time. Here he found it no less awkward for being encountered in a nobleman rather than a royal; and more particularly in view of the delicate nature of what it was now his duty to explain to him.

"I and the other member of the Faculty—" he began stiffly, but Humphrey waved that preamble aside and said with impatience:

"Now look here, sir, let us mince words no longer! I have been summoned back from Belgium with a peremptory haste which, I am persuaded, can only mean my father is grievously sick. I am also aware that it would go much against the pluck with him to send for me on his own account. Therefore, I conclude that the message was despatched on advice— on your advice, sir."

Doctor Knight looked grave. Discarding his air of pomposity as bidden, he inclined his head and murmured: "Aye, my lord, I ventured to send for you. Understand me: he took the palsystroke well—came out of it in as high croak as I've seen in any such case of his years. And I can say I am content now with his

response to our phlebotomy—though I vastly disliked
to cup him with the moon in this quarter. But,
unluckily, there is another complication: something
which pertains more to his mind than body, if you
follow, and which our recourse to valerian has as yet
served little to—"

Knight broke off what he was saying, startled by
the marked pallor which had suddenly invaded the
Earl's features. It happened to be a particular
speciality of his to study variations in skin colour,
and rarely did he note them with undue concern
since he was familiar with the superficial significance of a healthy complexion; indeed, he had written a dogmatic and voluminous paper on that very
subject. But now, for the first time, his firm conclusions wavered a little as the Earl—before his
eyes—ran a whole gamut of shades, right from a
boyish high pink down to positively Nabob-sallowness;
all in a few seconds that it took the candles on the
wall to waver and steady again in a puff of breeze
from the window. "My lord—" he began anxiously,
but Humphrey again interrupted him.

"His *mind*?" he said hoarsely. "What the deuce
d'you mean, his mind? Are you trying to prepare me
that my father is bound for a straight-waistcoat, sir?"

Knight at once responded with professional heart-
iness: "No, no, nothing of that nature, I do assure
you! It is merely that he appears to nourish some
inner disappointment, some gnawing regret or imaginary shame . . ." He made an odd, frustrated gesture
with his short arms, to convey his difficulty in
explaining such things to a mere nobleman who was
not a member of the Faculty. ". . . Doubtless it is
some trifling matter that he has repined upon—as I
have experienced on several past occasions with
such patients. But I repeat: his lordship is in no

danger of losing his reason, and I intended no such inference for one moment. It is true that he seems sometimes to be out of reason vexed—but mad? Oh no!"

He was puzzled when the look of torment in the Earl's eyes did not noticeably diminish after he had given him that reassurance. "So . . . not madness, then. *Gnawing regret,* eh? And *imaginary shame* . . . Those were your words, sir, were they not?" the young man mumbled, staring down at the many rings bedizening his hands.

"Well, yes," the doctor continued uncertainly. "As I said, it does occur sometimes in such cases. There is no physical, no apparent reason why they should not make a full recovery and become almost as they were before the palsystroke, except that their minds, from some strange cause, insist upon opposing the healing force," he finished roundly.

"Pray tell me, I must know . . . was he much overset by the—the few words that he and I exchanged when I first arrived today?"

Knight smiled his bland bedside smile. "Oh, be content on that head, my lord. I saw him an hour ago and he seemed then—well, perhaps a degree less prosperous than earlier. But I gave him a composer of mace-ale before Suddaby relieved me, and he was sleeping well when I left them both."

Deep feeling had made Humphrey forget that he was now discussing private family matters with a stranger. With a similar suspension of normal reserve, he now said urgently: "Listen—not to cut a wheedle with you—if I can—that is, if he and I could—well, I mean, now that I am home again, if he and I could but contrive not to come to cuffs all the time, do you suppose it might help him to—? You see

I cannot forbear the thought that I myself am the main cause of—"

He choked silent, feeling wetness in his eyes, and the society doctor regarded him in thoughtful silence for a few moments before replying.

He had met with quite enough fathers and sons in his several years of practice, both within noble households and in the larger fashionable world outside them, to be well aware of the constraints which that relationship could impose on the men concerned; and never with greater forcefulness than when one was the heir of the other.

He said gently: "I am sure you can be of the very greatest assistance to his mending, my lord. That was indeed the principal reason why I ventured to advise your return to Hoadoak."

"You were in the right," Humphrey said thickly. "Very right . . . All is not as it should be between us. We have never dealt well together since . . . before I was abroad. I blame myself . . ."

"As he blames himself likewise, I have little doubt, my lord. And now I shall leave you at last to your bed—and I prescribe that you sleep late in it tomorrow!"

He moved to the door, turning back to add kindly: "Are you intending to remove your own boots with the jack there, or do you desire me to send word that your man is to return to you?"

Humphrey, with difficulty, pulled his mind back to mundane matters. "No, I thank you. I am very accustomed to an absent valet after these last two years. Goodnight, sir—and I am obliged to you for confiding in me so frankly and so promptly."

Five

Perhaps Doctor Knight, having gained some insight into the character of the future Marquis of Cornford, decided to make similarly tactful representations to the present holder of the title. Whether that was the case or not, the Earl found his parent in more gracious mien when he spoke with him again the following day.

"My dear boy—" the sick man had begun, as soon as Humphrey entered the chamber, and struggling up a little higher on the pillows with a smile on his drawn face.

"Father . . . I collect you are going on better now," Humphrey responded, with only the slightest sardonic edge to that observation.

"I am, a trifle . . . I must straightway apologise to you: I cannot entirely recall how I greeted you upon your return home, my memory being all to pieces like so much else of me besides, but I dare swear I was unkind."

Humphrey moved forward impulsively to the chair by the bedhead, placing his fingers gently over the cold hand which lay on the counterpane. "Pay no heed to that, sir! I gave you a bear-garden jaw myself—you must have concluded the Tour had furnished me a damnably poor polish!"

The patient chuckled a little at that, until it brought on a racking cough. Reaching a glass of water to his lips for him, Humphrey said with renewed concern: "Knight said nothing to me of this cough you have, father."

"He has naught to say to *me* upon it, either," his parent finally managed to splutter. "Oh, I am out of patience with that cock-brained pair! First I am supposed to have suffered only the palsy—which was enough meat for old Suddaby to get his teeth into, but it wouldn't do for that nigmenog sawbones from town! *He* must then move Heaven and Earth to discover a 'complicating chill', which, once puffed up and nodded over by the two of them, proceeds, as they *say* they anticipated, to 'inflame my lungs'. Did you ever hear such fustian, Humphy, when none knew better than I that I was filled not with flames, but with polar ice? Next, doubtless because his inventiveness begins to flag, he and old slow-top Suddaby elect to cup me, if you please! Ah, the truth is plain enough to see under all their smoke, Humphy! I'm in the suds . . ."

"You don't appear so to me," Humphrey told him in soothing accents; and indeed, now that the coughing fit had subsided, Thomas Freen's vexation with his doctors had strengthened his voice almost to normal, and also improved his colour to a degree where he looked much the same choleric father whom he had stormily parted from two years since.

That silent reflection may have been divined by the patient, who now declared in a quieter, mournful tone: "I'll have you know that it was almost bellows to mend with me once . . ."

"Which, of course, was the prime reason why I was sent for, father."

"Damned fools!" snapped the patient, tacking around swiftly to find fault of a contrary nature. "Fishing you back from the Tour like hysterical—by the bye, Humphy, did you take the Netherlands when you was there?"

There was now a changed note in his voice which Humphrey recognised of old; and which, for the first time, he could respond to. He said: "Well enough, father. But after Italy—well, anywhere, anything after that would have been . . ."

The old Tourist in the bed nodded eagerly, studying his face. "Superfluous?" he prompted. "Satiety?"

"Neither one, sir, precisely: it was more that— well, I found I could hardly *see* Holland and Belgium, because my eyes, my spirit, was so crowded with what had gone before."

"Ah!" exclaimed his parent, on a long reflective sigh. "And that could be myself speaking, all those years ago after I was just returned from abroad. Of course, Humphy, there can be no true comparison, you apprehend. It was another world then, before the Frogs' revolt and then that curst fellow Bonaparte. The wonderful world I knew, whether abroad or here at home, lies in total ruin . . ."

"Of course, father," his son murmured dutifully, detecting a falter in the sick man's speech that owed more to his constitution than to lowering memories. He rose, saying with a smile: "I will come to you again after dinner, if you are not asleep by then."

"Pray do so—God bless you, my boy. Like your poor mother you have a—a forgiving nature."

Feeling heartened by this conversation, Humphrey

proceeded out of doors and was soon deep in talk with Harrow, the bailiff.

But that did not go as well as he had been hoping; for Harrow adopted a demeanour towards him which he had already encountered in some degree from the butler and the other senior servants: showing their awareness that the circumstances of his return necessitated some unbending of their old easy manner with him, but tempered by what he could only regard as a stupid and misplaced deference to his father. That, he knew, lay behind Harrow's evasiveness as soon as he tried to discuss estate matters of any importance with him; when any halfling with eyes in his head could see that many things at Hoadoak were crying out for proper attention, and not receiving it.

Suppressing his rising annoyance with the man, he made a further attempt to gain his confidence. "How is Mary, James? My God, but it seems two *hundred* years since I was last in your cot while she physicked me! Remember—after we'd dug that vixen out of Low Four-acre, and it took half my finger off for my pains? Look—I have the shortened remnant here still!"

But Harrow only smiled his stiff, withdrawn smile once again at that personal reminiscence. "Thank you, sir, she stays well. And of course I remember that day," he replied coolly.

Humphrey sighed in defeat. "Understand me, Jim—I am not wishful in any way to encroach, but I took out the stallion before breakfast and it soon became plain to me that if this place is to be brought about, then—"

"Brought about, sir?" echoed the bailiff in a tone of prickling resentment. "Am I to understand you find there has been *neglect* in your absence?" He paused, to draw a long indignant breath and add heatedly: "I know that my lord has made no complaint—not even the smallest direction. I think I may claim to possess his total confidence, being as I have now remained in his service, man and lad, for twenty-two years!"

Humphrey felt heat coming to his own face at this majestic rebuke, and said sharply: "Lord, take a damper, Jim!" But he was still more bewildered than annoyed. Turning on his heel, he strode back across the stable yard towards the house.

Coming in through the hall, with his Hessians making rather an agitated clatter on the floor, Philippa heard him from the morning room and called out to him to join her there before he put off his riding dress.

She was arranging early daffodil buds in a Venetian vase which their father had brought home long ago. She smiled as he entered; seeing him instinctively duck his head in the way of tall men in a strange place. Laughing, she told him: "You won't crack yourself on that lintel, Humph! One can tell how long you have been away from us!"

Then, noticing his expression as he cast himself into a chair, her smile faded and she said anxiously: "What now? I heard from father that you and he dealt extremely together this morning."

"Oh, I suppose so, Pip . . . But if it's not him I brangle with then it seems to be somebody else . . . I wrought with Harrow just now—quite to no purpose. I have the feeling that everyone here is, well, *different* with me: one would think I never had the managing of Hoadoak before I want away."

Not quite comprehending, she tried to rally him out of these low spirits. "Come, now, is that so very odd? You left here if not exactly a country gapeseed, then something not altogether unlike one—and then,

suddenly, two years later, reappear grown up in
every way and looking like Mr Brummell's continental twin! Of course they find you different—you
are different!"

"They never liked me above half," he muttered,
taking out his Roman quizzing-glass and staring
vaguely through the lens at an iron-mould spot upon
his wristband; not really listening to her. ". . . And
after that scandal—a deuced sight less. And it would
seem, sister, that it requires a deal of time to go by
before rustic servants change their opinions," he
declared, with an onset of the same bitterness that
she had hoped was not behind him.

Suddenly it came to her how mistaken he was;
though understandably so. "Humph—pray consider
the situation as it must appear to them from the
Room. If you had only seen father last week I'm sure
you would appreciate what I'm saying . . . He was so
very ill then, and of course they all knew. And what
with both the doctors being so full of professional
consequence and secrecy—of course they have all
been expecting the worst to befall! I confess to you,
two days before you came back to us I did myself . . .
Oh Humphy, you can have *no notion* what a terrible
time it has been for everybody at Hoadoak!"

And, crushing the luckless stalks which were at
that moment in her grasp, Lady Philippa had run
awkwardly forward across the room and sobbed
abandonedly into her brother's cheek; just as she
had longed to do when she first set eyes on him
again.

He gently detached her. "Now then, dearest
Pippy—I can see I have been a gudgeon where your
feelings are concerned: but as for Harrow and Chenson
and the rest of our host of barnacles—you will not
convince me that they regard my return with

unleavened joy, for I just shan't believe you!"

"Perhaps not," she sniffed, fetching a handkerchief from the pocket of her sarsnet apron, "but it is only because they are unsettled. They all, from Chenson down to Kitchen Tommy, divine that you may become 'my lord' to them quite soon, in the sense they can still think only of him—don't you see? Try not to give way to silly crotchets!"

"Hm," he said, dropping the glass on its riband and getting up to move across to the window overlooking the fishpond. "Who can possibly apprehend the working of servitors' minds?—not I, to be sure."

She almost made a short answer to that haughty remark, until she caught the plaintive note in his voice and realised that he was still feeling hurt by the lack of spontaneous warmth from the Kentish folk; who had known him, in many cases, from babyhood.

"That stew is silted on the north bank," he remarked next, peering through the window. "I wonder which jackanapes is too 'unsettled' to dig it out, eh? I own I am growing very weary of this lamentable situation I find here—and that's not all!"

"No?" Lady Philippa said nervously.

"No! I am perturbed about you and the twins."

"About us?" she exclaimed in astonishment. "But we're all perfectly stout, I assure you!"

He seemed not to hear this reassurance. "Yes—you! Not only do I come home to find the estate in what would be poor case for a landlord with half father's blunt, and sorely in need of his eye and hand, but you three, also, are scarcely up to the rig, if I may say so! Unless I am much mistaken, you are all set fair to become ape-leaders!"

"Oh . . ." she said faintly, sitting down and staring. "Are we, now?"

"Aye, I fear so," he continued remorselessly, raising his quizzer once more to examine the watery view beyond the window. "Take your own situation first: what kind of a push has our aunt made on your account, with several opportunities to bring the thing off, and franked, I collect, handsomely enough by Papa? I will tell you what I think—a damnably poor push!"

"Aunt Clem did her best!" she protested crossly. (Though feeling extremely unnerved by this further new side of her brother, which had taken her by surprise even more than had his foreign ways.) "You ought to reflect that she is old now—and that it is very trying for a female of her years to be up night after night for weeks on end, due to the exigencies of the Season."

"I do not doubt it. I do beg leave to doubt that she is still fitted for such an onerous task—and I feel more doubtful still that she could be entrusted with Nell's and Margaret's come-outs."

"But who else is to oblige us, then? Aunt Clem—however much you may denigrate her—has the highest of connexions." She gazed at the back of his head in sudden dire suspicion. "Humph—if you are thinking that I would *stoop for one moment* to apply to Henrietta Worsby for her patronage, you may think again! Our family may happen to be woefully short of that rare species of chaperon in this particular generation—as you would know if you were not a man!—but I *would not stand with that odious creature if her hatband was chock-full of Almack's vouchers right the way around it!*" she declared in a passion.

Her brother laughed deprecatingly. "Oh no, Pip,

you are quite abroad there! From what I recall of her I would never wish that particular kinswoman upon you! No, that was not my purpose at all in raising the matter."

"Well!" she cried in exasperation, tiring of the sight of the back of him and coming to stand at his side in the embrasure. "What purpose had you, then?—other, perhaps than to reduce my own self-esteem and scarcely enhance that in which I hold my aunt and sisters?"

His profile grinned wryly as that neat shaft sank home. "No need to rip up at me . . . listen, I have a scheme. When I was in Milan, I learned it was quite the thing there for a young-ish gentleman—a brother, say, to sponsor a young lady—perhaps his sister—into Roman society, providing that—"

Her scornful laugh cut across him. "Indeed it is certainly *not* the thing in Duke Street, Humphrey!"

He gripped her arm in a restraining way, continuing earnestly: "Provided that his duties are shared with a suitable lady of mature years."

"That makes it a degree more sensible, I suppose, and not altogether the outside of enough! But not five minutes ago you were objecting to just such a 'lady of mature years'—in the form of our Aunt Clemmy!"

"I might well revise my opinion of her, were she pulling in tandem, Italian style, as I propose," he countered stubbornly.

"*Pulling in tandem!* I beg you, let us leave this subject before I, too, become miffed with your distempered foreign freaks! Let me merely say that your scheme would not answer—and for all manner of reasons outside your knowledge: one other, which perhaps you could apprehend, being that Aunt Clem would certainly not consent to anything so ram-

shackle! She may have lacked success in her endeavours to fix an interest on my behalf, but I would
be the last to say she is not the highest stickler who
ever led an eligible through that modish maze."

He shrugged, acknowledging a defeat on that particular battleground, and tucked his glass finally
away; in its place thumbing open a large snuff-box,
ornamented on its lid with a classical *grisalle* design
on mother-of-pearl. "To the devil with Aunt Clem—
I've just thought of the very person who could deal
with this matter to admiration," he said ominously,
taking a meditative pinch.

"I am not sure I should listen to you any longer on
this head," she told him with a strained smile,
"but—very well, I shall—for a few seconds more, at
least! No, I mean at *most!*"

He took another teasingly long sniff. Then: "I
chanced to ride by the Dower House this morning,"
he remarked idly; but that apparently inconsequen-
tial remark was lost in a gusty peal of laughter from
beside him.

"You mean *Grandmama!*—and *you*, pulling me in
tandem, Italian style? My God, I would liefer resign
to become an ape-leader any day! I vow that I would
die of whoops at the very first squeeze the pair of you
supervised!"

"I saw her face at the little arched window as I rid
by—I collect the old griffin goes on as strong as
ever?" he said with every sign of seriousness. "And
not even you, Pip, can hold that she is not of the very
first rank."

She goggled at him, realising that levity was
indeed entirely absent from both his voice and features. "But—but she is *ages* older than Aunt Clem!
And surely you cannot have forgotten that she is
also . . . mad!"

"Pooh, that's surely pitching it too rum: of course I have not spoken with her since the time of that damned duel, but she was by no means queer in her attic then—strange, I would concede, but by no means mad."

"Well, perhaps I shouldn't have called her that," she allowed grudgingly. "Anyway, she would never consent. Not only did she abjure the fashionable world when you were still in short coats, but she has remained incarcerated there in the Dower House, with only her old pet footman for company, ever since you left us."

"But you and father and the girls have called upon her during that interval, no doubt?" Humphrey said with a trace of concern which his next words explained. "She was the sole person—bar you, of course, Pip—who showed me the least understanding over that Hipsley affair, and I have always had a soft spot for her from that time hence."

"Don't be idiotish!—of course we've called on her! I go over there myself about once every month, and would do so more often except that Granny dislikes anything more frequent and makes that very plain if one forgets not to go! As for her sympathy for you, Humph—I am surprised you haven't detected the simple reason for that: when she was young, it was not so extraordinary, or unpardonable, for bewigged gentlemen to wave swords at each other, and perhaps draw a little exciting blood upon their silly wristruffles, and stamp their bare feet in a great show of temper!"

Philippa was aware that these last words carried a sting with them, but felt he had merited it through his own blunt observations. But, to her surprise, he seemed indifferent to her opinion of duellists and merely replied: "Good! I find I approve of Grandmama's rule of strictly limited at-homes: by the reckoning of one a month, I calculate she should be pleased to receive twenty-four such visits from me, very soon, to catch the rest of you up!"

And, chuckling in a self-satisfied way at that brilliant piece of wit, he marched from the room; leaving Lady Philippa a prey to extreme apprehension.

With the same determined straighforwardness of approach, Humphrey raised both the matters which he had broached with Philippa when he spoke with his father again after dinner that day.

He found the old man to be still improved and still polite to him; though his own opening remarks went some way to imperilling that new civility.

"Ah, sir, I am glad you are awake! I have now had a chance to look over most of the southern land, and consulted with Harrow, and it seems to me most vital that—"

"Eh? Harrow? *Consulted?*" said the Marquis, on a dangerous rising inflexion; and Humphrey, belatedly realising his mistake, rushed in headlong in an attempt to explain it away.

"Ah, sir, when I use the word *consult*, I mean merely to signify that he and I chanced to unsaddle together after I was riding, and naturally we fell to jawing over what so plainly needs to—"

"Harrow addressed you, did he, my boy?" the supine figure murmured with disconcerting acuteness.

"Well, not precisely, no, but—"

"Then, ergo, you must have addressed Harrow," said his parent with classical satisfaction; that conclusion did not, however, appear to please him generally. He fixed a wintry gaze upon his heir and observed: "Harrow has been with me for twenty-two years."

"Aye—so he has reminded me himself."

The Marquis laughed a little at that disclosure, and coughed rather more. The proof of his bailiff's faithful intransigence restored his good humour, however, and when the fit was over he merely croaked: "Please to leave the men alone, Hump, there's a good boy. Give them time to know you again. They all know their work—if they are left to do it."

"My sentiments exactly, sir! But what I take leave to question is whether . . ."

But, fortunately, this time he also took due note of the kindling light in my lord's eyes, and held his tongue; then passed on unwillingly to the other, secondary subject he wished to raise with him aside from the estate matters. "The women, sir—the three girls—are you sanguine that my aunt is, er, capable enough when she takes them up to the Village?"

Here he was on much firmer ground, knowing that my lord had never entertained a high regard for his late wife's sister. Indeed, such expressions as 'fusty tabby'; 'ninnyhammer'; 'wet goose'; 'widgeon' and the like had been known to pass his lips on more than one occasion whilst his lady was still alive and present: and afterwards, the epithets heaped upon her extant sister had grown more colourful still.

"Clemmy, you mean? Capable? Hah!" he now said expressively. Then: "What hare are you running now, Humphy? What ails the girls that I don't know of?"

"Well, I collect that Pippy has grown rather tired of undergoing the Season: tho' perhaps you did not know that."

"The devil I did! *Tired,* you say? Why should *she*

be tired of it if *I* ain't, Humphy? Damme, I've stood
the nonsense for that chit to the tune of I don't know
how much! Her come-out pearls were from Rundells,
you know!" he declared aggrievedly.

"She does not say so—but I do, sir—that our aunt
has made a sad mull of the business."

"Oh, very like . . . but what can be done to remedy
it? That ninny-hammer is supposed to be arm-in-
armly with those who count, you know . . ."

"And yet, sir—not one eligible offer in two Seasons?" Humphrey persisted.

His father stirred restively in the bed, considering
in silence what he had told him. Presently he said:
"You're mindful of the other two, eh, when their turn
comes presently?"

"I am. Not but what it is so wonderful if Pip don't
take well: I find since my return, sir, that she has a
certain *humorous* style with her which would never
do in Italy. But that aside, I'd vow Aunt Clem has a
deal to answer for. I confess I'm uneasy, lest she
blights the twins also when they go to her."

"But who else to apply to, my boy?"

"I thought . . . perhaps the Dowager?"

"You thought *what*!" exclaimed the patient, sitting upright and staring wildly, in a manner that
would have much intrigued Doctor Knight had that
fashionable practitioner then been at the bedside.

While taken aback by this alarming response,
Humphrey this time stuck to his guns. "I'm persuaded Grandmama might consent to such a scheme
—if I represented to her."

"*My mother!*—go out in Society again!—after God
knows how long?" my lord gasped in amazement.
"One more word on *that* head, Hump, and I shall
think you are either disguised or unhinging, damme,
if I won't!"

Now, for the first time in this conversation, Humphrey employed a degree of cunning. With a sigh of agreement he murmured: "You know best, sir ... and, in any event, perhaps the old lady never was in the Almack's touch ... I see now it was a buffleheaded notion."

"*Almack's?*" the patient rasped in his ear. "*That* fribble parlour? Good God, boy, she was the Queen of Carlisle's Club in her day! *And* of the Pantheon! When Society *was* Society! When town *was* town—and not full of cits and mushrooms and what you calls your 'demi-beaux'! To speak of *my mam* in the same breath as *Almack's!*" And here Thomas Freen ceased to speak himself; merely uttering a throaty whistling sound which, nevertheless, expressed much the same vehement sense of outrage as had his foregoing remarks.

"Even so," his son pursued, after a moment's cautious silence, "what with her constitution, which could scarcely—"

"Like an ox, always was," my lord said huffily. "Did I never tell you, Hump, of the time when she swam out a mile from Scarborough, one icy day in February of 'Fifty-five?—No, damme, I mean February of 'Fifty-*eight*, don't I?"

He broke off for a moment to laugh, and to cough, uproariously. Then he whispered: "The most shockin' thing that was ever seen there! Mam did it for a wager—on the high tide! Climbed out trailin' ropes of seaweed off her long heavy dress (none of your flimsy ankle-shows then, my boy!) on to a little fisher-boat—damned nigh capsizing 'em! For she was a big woman, Humphy, as her bones tell you even now."

In fact, Humphrey had heard several times, and as many versions, of his grandmother's famous youthful prank at the seaside. His own sceptical view of it was that the old lady had probably fallen in by accident off the promenade, then just floundered about in a conspicuous style until she was picked up. But, prudently, he aired none of this theory as his parent happily recounted and embellished the piece of family history yet again.

A circumstance now came to his aid which could not have occurred to him: one of the things which had rancoured the Marquis, whilst he was passing through the crisis of his illness, was a disagreeable apprehension that the venerable old lady across the lawn there (hubble-bubble though she might be) was now in a fair way to survive himself. And, tossing fitfully in the real or imaginary humours diagnosed by his physicians, the reason for that likely outcome had seemed obvious enough: *she* did nothing all day and night but rest her strength; whereas *he* always had 'Change to repine at, or Politics, or Humphy, or the estate, the house, the horses, the three girls . . . It was scarcely surprising that the comfortable old lady (apart from being hubble-bubble) was as sound as a bell by comparison . . .

Such sickly fancies and resentments as these had now been dispelled by his regaining of a little strength; but the thought still come to him that it might indeed be more *natural* for his mother to sometimes emerge from that dark old house of hers, instead of staying there cosseted for evermore.

He rubbed the white bristles upon his chin, which his man had not liked to shave any closer during his illness, and said with an air of heavy playfulness: "You think you can bring her round your thumb as you always can me, eh, you scoundrel? Well then, try at it! But it'll never fadge—you're forty years too late!"

Six

Miss Chance, the consequential and very expensive dresser whom Lord Cornford had engaged for his eldest daughter at the optimistic time of her come-out, was not pleased, late the next afternoon, to be charged by her lady to stand spying by the dressing-chamber window. Strong disapprobation showed in every line of her squat back as she looked down from there as bidden.

"Well?" Philippa demanded from the chair before the looking-glass, awkwardly brushing her own hair and with two dressing pins sticking from her mouth. "Is he still within?"

"It would appear so," Miss Chance replied in an arctic accent. "It is—hard for me to—to peer through the shrubbery from this—this position."

The dresser's speech was often larded in this style with genteel and querulous ambiguities, but now Philippa was far too overwrought to smooth her down in the way she knew was required of her. Instead she mumbled distractedly through the pins: "I can't understand why he's so long ensconced with her, surely it can't mean that—"

"Ah!" the dresser remarked suddenly, straightening.

"Yes?" Philippa put down the hair-brush and half-rose.

"Oh . . . no, it's nothing . . . merely that disgusting old man appearing outside to sweep out the porch—for the first time in years, by the look of that pile of leaves."

Miss Chance, for all her habitual ill-temper, was not exaggerating the case when she had complained of the difficulties in her way to complying with Philippa's request; for the shrubbery around the Dower House—as though reflecting its two occupants' retiring dispositions—had rioted over the last few decades to form a barrier of foliage, so that the house itself had become almost invisible from the Hoadoak mansion. Earlier, that afternoon, both ladies had observed the considerable difficulty with which the Earl had found and forced his way down the gravel path to the little Gothick porch of the house. However, once inside, he had vanished from their gaze for so long that Philippa had moved crossly away to her mirror, leaving Miss Chance to serve as lone sentinel.

That arrangement, however, had its drawbacks for her too, as she was discovering. "Where have you put the French gold?" she now asked, rummaging clumsily in the chest through her gowns.

"In the middle, betwixt the red stuff and the muslin spot," the dresser told her, still eyeing the Dower House with an air of martyrdom.

"I can't find it!"

"I am surprised, in any event, that you should think of the gold trim for an evening at home with your brother," Miss Chance said dispassionately. "Perhaps I may have placed it next that new low waist you so admore . . . oh, I perceive I had best attend to it myself!" she exclaimed, seizing upon this excuse to step back into the body of the room.

And thus it came about that a few seconds later, despite his sister's suspicious and well-organised observation of his movements, Humphrey was able to quit the Dower House unscrutinised; making it impossible for her to know at once (as she was sure she would have been able, from one glance at his guilty expression), exactly what jingle-brained scheme had been hatched in the little house through the trees.

In fact, had she known what had just been decided there she would have become far too flustered and angry to continue dressing for dinner, either with or without the chilling and undeferential aid of Miss Chance. ·

A totally different style of servant had greeted Humphrey when he emerged dripping from the over-grown bushes, and trod upon the rotten wood of the Dower House porch. The door was pulled open with a grand flourish and a high and reedy voice trumpeted at him: "My lord, may I make so bold as to welcome you to your ancestral home once more—late-expressed tho' I fear that sentiment must now appear!"

"Er, obliged to you, Grimes . . ." Humphrey responded, putting up his glass to eye with both caution and recognition the odd figure standing before him.

Once—a long time ago—this personage had been a strikingly handsome first footman; not only here in the country, but with a lengthy period of prior service at Cornford House. Even now in advancing age the bowed tie wig of his youth was still carefully set upon his head and meticulously powdered; but a thin, bony and yellow face now grinned at Humphrey in place of the plump rosiness of countenance which he recalled dimly from childhood memories. Gone, too, was the ancient puce-coloured livery which even Grandmama (so he had heard from Philippa) had lately decided was no longer suitable. The old footman was now clad in short Hessians, long breeches, and with a spencer over his jacket, and most of him looked like an only slightly outmoded rustic squire.

"Shall I cause enquiries to be made, my lord, to determine whether my mistress is indoors?" the ex-footeman proposed with the utmost gravity, after vouchsafing him several other archaic civilities.

Humphrey—who now noticed uneasily that Grimes's faded eyes had a disconcerting glitter in their depths—hastily removed the smile which this final absurdity had provoked, and nodded his assent with some relief.

And, after Grimes's nice judgement of the proper interval, with enormous punctilio he was presented to his grandmother.

The last time he had seen her here, he had been far too overborne with his own dire situation to discern much more than the fact that she appeared still much the same quaint and solitary old woman who chose (perhaps understandably) to perpetuate the manners and customs of her prime. But now he grasped almost at once that, since the last visit he had paid her, what could then have been dismissed as affectation was now hardened to something stronger and more pronounced. Indeed, regarding the pair of them, as the strange old servant bowed and scraped his way out backwards from the room, Humphrey began to comprehend more easily Philippa's mirth when he first suggested the change of chaperon to her.

However, having surmounted the major obstacle

of winning his father's consent to the scheme, he was damned if he was going to cry craven on it now . . . Forcing his eyes downward from the hypnotic towering summit of the old lady's white and whitened coiffure, to her rather large and wrinkled face about a yard beneath, he gave a determined cough and said: "I trust I find you stout, madam, after being so long away . . ."

But despite his resolution, when she continued to stare at him bleak-eyed and without speaking, his gaze floated up again in embarrassed fascination: he saw that the lower part of her hair resembled a man's wig (rather like Grimes's), whilst the upper, raised on half-concealed cushions, terminated in a lofty peak like a grenadier's cap with a bouquet on top of it. The rest of her still sizable frame was covered with an almost disintegrating example of that species of huge-hipped gown which he knew from many of the large portraits which hung in the Hoadoak gallery: though there the funny old dresses always seemed new and alive to him, despite their flat artistic representation; whereas here his grandparent sat now looking a perfect likeness of dusty death.

This morbid fancy was sharply dispelled when the old lady finally found her tongue. "Master Humphy again!" she declared with severity, blinking at him with her bright dark eyes that were intelligent, and yet subtly not so.

"Ahem, ma'am, I fear it is every bit of two years since I—"

"Not two weeks, you say! Speak up, Master Humphy, you're on my right side, mind you! Speak up! Aye—not two minutes by your own admission! Aren't you yet sensible that I don't care for you, or for any Family, in *regular two minute doses,* eh? La,

I'm fond of you all well enough, but I do like my own fireside to myself and my own man about me and . . . where *is* that dratted man gone off to now, Master Humphy? —*I* never dismissed him! *Drat him!*"

Whereupon the old lady—grown suddenly and alarmingly purple-faced—almost swayed over sideways in her chair, so lustily and furiously did she haul upon the nearby bell-rope.

When Grimes returned—with an alacrity that Humphrey could not but compare favourably with the time it seemed to take the present Hoadoak servants to answer to summons—he was greeted with the fond words: "Whopstraw! I shall turn you off at the twelve-month!" There followed a severe rakedown, which, while it appeared to perturb its object not a whit, increasingly convinced Humphrey that he had made a ridiculous mistake in thinking to enlist the old termagant's aid; and when Grimes had left them again he got up from his chair and muttered something of going himself now.

"What, boy?—I really shall give that rascal his *congé,* he don't think I've the heart to but that's where he's—*sit down,* Master Humphy! You must want *something* of me, stripling! Or was it just sight of me pretty face, then?"

"Er, I was persuaded, ma'am—but no matter now . . ."

"You was persuaded *what,* thatchgallows?"

"I beg your pardon?" he stuttered, in shaken order.

"Well, *ain't* you a regular thatchgallows?" she demanded shrilly. "Didn't you pink that officer and have to *run off to France,* eh? I shall ask you once more: *what d'you want of me?*"

He eyed her a shade differently. It appeared that her memory, at least, still served her passably well if in crooked style; not the whole of her mind was all about by any means. He cleared his throat, feeling a great fool, but forced out the words: "It came to me you might assist to bring the girls into fashion."

She fell broodingly silent, her unreliable eyes taking in her grandson more particularly. He was wearing morning dress of dark superfine, breeches and top-boots for this call, not having cared to expose either the Italian Hessians, or the white pantaloons, to her inspection and comments. Finally she pursed her cerise lips and said: "How could I, Master Humphy, when there's no fashion to bring 'em into, eh?"

Supposing from this reply that her mind had given way once more, he again began to quit his chair; but then apprehended that her words were sardonic rather than maniacal, and half-heartedly subsided. "Just so, ma'am—but to young Nell and Meg it is a different matter, and I sincerely wish that they could be better served than by my aunt."

"Oh—that fussocks!" said the old lady with crushing scorn. "She ain't got sixpence to scratch with and she resides in *Grosvenor Place*! What did you and Cornford expect her to bring off from that situation, eh?—and when charged with that gel who's as big and idiotish as you are to be rid of!"

Forcing back the immediate retort that was provoked by this unkindness to Philippa and himself, he replied in level tones: "I doubt myself it is left too late now for Pippy. My concern is principally for the other two."

"*Them* little fatties!" She shook her coiffure so violently that the whole toppling creation took a dangerous side-slip until her hand went to steady it. "The money would do better staying in his Consols than spent on them little piglets—who, as anyone can see, won't do for *that* market!" she cackled merrily.

"If that is your opinion then I—"

"*Sit down!* Pray, how many more times do I have to tell you? Resty boy . . . What do the fatties want, anyway, just a ball or two?"

"I have not asked them what they want," he said in some bewilderment. "But I think Pippy hoped for Almack's until it became clear that Aunt Clem had no entrée. I suppose the girls would wish for the same."

By this time he was feeling extremely regretful that he had not confined his attentions to estate matters upon returning home; since however much his father and the servants might resent and obstruct him in that direction, at least a man knew where he was amongst such safe things as drainage and Corn Laws and Property Tax; whereas on this present undertaking he seemed to be fair game for raillery and abuse from all quarters.

He had expected that his last remark would elicit some further colourful disparagement of her younger grandchildren from the old belle; but she took much the same unusual line as had her son upon the mention of Almack's famous Rooms. "That's all I signified when I said a ball or two," she snapped contemptuously, fanning herself.

He looked at her in mystification, wondering if she was being mad again or—? "Are you saying—let me be clear—that you possess an entrée there?"

"Good God, I should *suppose that I do!*" she told him vehemently, and with a brief return of suffusion to her features. "If that Jersey chit is still alive—which she should be, as she can scarcely be no age at all yet—or even if she is dead, there is that other foreign one named . . . Something-hazy, I collect. Only conceive of *her* disobligin' *me!*" she exclaimed dourly.

Humphrey gaped at her. Unversed as he was in fashionable matters outside his beloved Italy, even he had heard vaguely of the names of the six great ladies who ruled the roast at Almack's Club; including those of Lady Jersey and the Princess Esterhazy. "Grandmama," he said recklessly, leaning forward to touch her robust, unwithered hand, "would you chaperon the three of them this time—please?"

"La, I don't go into Society any more, Master Humphy."

But those discouraging words were uttered with a kind of teasing undertone which several other gentlemen (now mostly deceased) apart from her grandson would have recalled with a severe pang, had they been present in spirit at her latest tête-à-tête. And Humphrey, as eager to persuade her as had been every other member of that ghostly company in his day, suddenly saw how to clinch it with the old girl. "You would not lack support in the endeavour, Granny, for it is my every intention to play a major part myself in securing good offers for Philippa and the twins," he told her earnestly.

Strangely enough, this intelligence did not receive the enthusiastic assent he had expected from her. In fact, Sarah Freen merely said grumpily: "Eh? What fresh gammon is this? *You* find them offers? Oh, I don't say you can't do the pretty when you wish to, after being abroad your ton seems good enough. But you, Master Humphy, will leave the offers to me!"

He made a further patient attempt to explain to her some of the admirable ways that Latin courtship was conducted; but had to abandon it in the face of her obvious disinterest, and coarse old-fashioned humour. But at least she finally consented to the main scheme; and, he was confident, would very likely come about to his own proposed role when he had a chance to demonstrate its soundness in practice.

Upon leaving her, he was just in time to express his heartfelt thanks to Doctor Knight, whose large and costly carriage, and team of high-bred greys, had been brought out from the stables and was then drawn up by the portico; about to remove him to another wealthy patient. The Marquis's condition—as he now informed his son—had improved so far beyond all expectations that in his judgement the Family Practitioner was now well able to oversee the case unaided.

Humphrey, with a renewal of the sense of gratitude he had first felt towards the shrewd and kind society doctor on the night of his return, stood on the gravel until the prime turn-out was set in motion, then went upstairs to attend to a certain matter and dress for dinner.

That occasion, pleasant enough though it was for him following upon the good outcome with his grandmother, and the cheering valediction from Knight, was something of an ordeal for Lady Philippa.

This was to have been the first time when her reunited family (bar of course their father upstairs) could sit down together for dinner, and she had accordingly urged Chenson and the cook to do their best. Mr Leach had responded marvellously: never had she tasted such lobsters from his hand since her distant memories of Cornford House. For the succession of dull country dinners at six, prepared ad nauseam, had discouraged the cook and gradually—so she had supposed—reduced his skills so that she had lately grown to expect very little from him above the level of haricots or escallops. And, later, a pastry case was presented which made her give an involuntary cry of appreciation, at first sight of the neat dressing of partridges and dried salmon. Even the Tourist, whilst regretting that Leach could not turn out an Italian salad, pronounced his efforts as being 'bang up to the knocker for plain English cookery.'

So it was not on account of the fare that she felt herself growing more and more irritated. The cause was simple enough: this first family dinner had been arranged before she had caught wind of Humphrey's plans concerning the Dowager; and now it was trying her patience beyond all bounds to be forced to sit there, exchanging girlish chatter with Nell and Meg, while their brother grinned to himself so smugly, and in such a sinister fashion; when all the time she was longing for the girls and the servants to be otherwhere, so she could put to him the several leading questions that were uppermost in her mind. She had a dread suspicion that her worst fears had already been outdistanced.

When the meal was over and the girls rose, she suddenly rebelled against the prospect of yet more vapid talk over the tea-tray. Beckoning crossly to Chenson, she told him: "Do you bring me some ratafia with his lordship's port, if you please."

Chenson was not of the formidable species of butler. He was a slim and easy-going man in his 'fifties with very blue, rather friendly eyes; very popular in the Room and possessing a rare turn for decorum without starchiness which made him equally appreciated by my lord. So it vexed Philippa more than she could express to see those vivid blue eyes now wavering uncertainly away from hers to seek confirmation of her instruction from Humphrey.

"Did you hear me?—ratafia!" she repeated fiercely, and this time Chenson bowed and withdrew after the girls.

Humphrey gave a sophisticated chuckle once the

door was closed behind the butler. "Now that, sister, could well have been my grandmother addressing her aged companion this afternoon!" he observed dryly. "One sees that you are her relation after all, despite the spleen you vent upon each other!"

That last remark did little to soften her expression as she asked in grim tones: "What did you and she prose together?—out with it, now!"

But he was able to preserve his maddening silence on that subject for a little while longer as Chenson returned with the decanter, and also bearing a small glassful which he set, with a rather wounded flourish, before Philippa.

When he closed the door on them finally she burst out in passion: "*Now,* you will please tell me what you've been brewing with that old witch or I'll—!"

"Splendid news, Pip," he interrupted with a bland, kindly air, sipping the port and rolling it affectedly round his mouth. "Ugh! Father's cat-lap don't improve, I must say ... When I was in—"

"What is your 'splendid news', pray?"

"Oh, that: the old woman will lend us her countenance, Pip. I fancied she might. She and I dealt famously!"

"Oh, you did, did you ..." she said between her teeth, glowering at him over the polished table.

"Indeed yes. She is happy not only to introduce the twins into fashion, as I besought her, but also to undertake the repair of Aunt Clem's bumble-bathing with your own case."

"How—how very kind!" Philippa choked upon her ratafia.

Ignoring—or perhaps unaware of—this response he continued blithely: "Yes: and the matter of Almack's I'm persuaded can also be left in her hands since—"

"Oh, I am out of all patience with you both!" Philippa cried out, replacing her glass on the table so firmly that the stem almost cracked. "I collect she hinted you about her bosom-bows at Court, did she not? —all of them buried these last twenty years or more! My God, I thought after being abroad you had acquired *some* sense at least!"

He stared at her in astonishment, plainly hurt, so that her anger seemed to spread outwards even further to encompass herself. For she had so particularly wished for this evening to be a pleasure for him—yet here they were disputing already. Even if he had deserved it, with his blundering interference, she was sorry now and tried to make amends. She said more quietly: "Humph—do but consider the effect that old creature would have if she were placed in charge of us three: that hair reeking of tallow!—those stiff silks and brocades!—those beyond anything mouse-skin eyebrows!—birds and Chinamen romping all over her hoop gowns!—that Babylonian head of hers, nodding at the poor Queen!—those fearful feathers, drooping . . . And, aside from all that, she is also chuck-full of outdated Whiggish notions of every kind! I beg you, Humph, try to see that taken altogether she would be *odious!*"

He looked a little stunned, as she had hoped he would, by this catalogue of faults, but rallied stoutly. "Ay, all true enough, I daresay. But Pip—she does have a direct entrée to Almack's, either through Lady Jersey or else the Princess."

Now it was Philippa's turn to be taken aback. "Mere mad talk!" she scoffed uncertainly. "Tho' I concede that those two are not dead yet—they would have been still in leading-strings when *she* was raking!"

"Come now, Pippy, she ain't as old as all that! I

believe she really does have the entrée—and I am not so much a greenhead as you evidently think. And besides, Almack's is by no means all that she can put in your way!"

Resolving to pass his continually jarring mode of expression, she replied with a weary sigh: "Well, what else, then?"

He paused impressively, to deliver what he knew must clinch it with her. "She says she will not stoop so low as to hire a town house."

"Will she not . . . then that ends this fustian!"

He shook his head, beaming. "—But insists that father opens Mount Street to her!"

She stared with incredulity. "Open *Cornford Huse*? As if he would! That does terminate old Sarah's part in our fortunes, most certainly!"

His smile was insufferable in its smugness. "No: I represented to him just before I came down—and he will comply with her condition!"

Seven

Hoadoak was a solid house built in Queen Anne's
reign, where quiet voices rarely penetrated through
any of the thick walls or doors. But at least one of
the voices emanating from the dining-room had not
been quiet for some time; and the ears of the two
damsels in the drawing-room had been strained to
catch every word.

When, at last, a rather deafening silence had
fallen upon their elders, Lady Ellen rose stiffly from
her unseemly crouch at the door and bounced herself
down hastily once again upon the sofa. Gulping a
swallow of luke-warm tea, she declared in a rush:
"Well! By Jupiter! What d'you—come back here
quick, Meggy, or they'll catch us!—what do *you*
think of all that amazingness!"

Lady Margaret, although only seventeen, had a
more practical disposition than her twin's. Resum-
ing her seat with dignity she said in a thoughtful
way: "Two things—one bad and one good." She then
paused to make elegant use of the silver pot, in the
manner of her poor mama; whom by now she could
only remember through a few such associations.

"*Bad?* What can you mean? To me it sounds above anything great!"

"Grandmama, in London, could be vastly bad, Nell! Surely even you can see that!—I'd vow Pippy does."

"Oh, fiddle-faddle!" declared her exuberant sister. "Humph plainly intends to squire us too, and besides, what has any of that to say when one thinks of *having Cornford House for our come-outs*! Confess, glumpish one!—you're every bit as up in the boughs as I am!"

"Of course I'm excited," allowed Lady Margaret; though without much appearing it. Rather, her dark brows were pulled together in a considering frown. "Do try to compose yourself before they come in—stop slopping those dregs, and have another proper cup, do!" she adjured her hoydenish twin, angling the spout more prettily still in front of her.

"I shall wear my white figured crape for the first home assembly," Ellen ran on unheeding. ". . . At least, I did *think* that I might, to go with Papa's pearl drops, but now I am in a doubt—is it grand enough?"

"If I possessed a bran complexion I should very likely resign myself on all occasions to either straw or jonquil," observed the mature young miss with the tea-pot. She began to speculate further on this theme, expressing the belief that if her own neck was a shade squat (fortunately not the case), so that ill-chosen pearl drops tended to hang all about one's shoulders, then she, personally, would have the good sense to leave them boxed at all times. But before this was more than half-expressed, in her sweet musing tones, the air was rent with a robust cry of "*Pig!*", and her sister arrived simultaneously beside her in a small wing chair, fists flailing.

For a brief moment Lady Margaret's developing sense of decorum caused her to suffer being pummelled in silent frustration and restraint. Then, however, a particularly wild blow made her gasp; casting all such inhibitions aside, battle was now enjoined with a squealing whole-heartedness from both parties which was a sad reflection on the finish which had been applied to them during the last year or so.

Not surprisingly, the chair rocked first upon one leg and then another; and the tea-pot spout—now employed by Margaret as a crude weapon—issued a brown arc which fell upon the carpet, followed hard upon by both damsels, and at the precise second when a tight-lipped Philippa swept into the room ahead of her brother.

"*Girls!*" she snapped at them awfully, "is *this* an example of the comportment to be expected from you shortly in town? If so, I'd liefer persuade Papa that his money should stay funded! Do you *get up*, the pair of you!" she commanded, with an anger she knew to be disproportionate to the offence.

Lady Margaret, while doing as she was bidden, had it upon the tip of her small pink tongue to wonder if their Papa was not now perfectly resigned, in any event, to the expenditure of his blunt upon lost causes of that nature; although she did not quite dare, on account of Philippa's stormy face, to say that. Lady Ellen bounded up resiliently and blurted to nobody in particular: "Oh, I—I am so *very* pleased with . . . everything!" And she almost choked from the necessity not to elaborate further.

Philippa glanced at her, biting her lip as she realised that of course the girls had been listening to their talk in the dining-room. But it was impossible for her to resist Ellen's beaming young countenance,

and her own features softened as she murmured:
"I see you already know the whole ..." She half-
turned ruefully towards Humphrey. "And I see also
that I am hopelessly outvoted in my view of the
matter!"

He gave an indulgent chuckle, raising his Roman
glass on its long riband to regard each young sister
in turn. "I fancy you are, Pip," he declared, putting it
away with an air of finality and taking a macaroon
from the tray.

With the arrival of the month of April, and some
seasonable spring weather over the Kentish countryside, Lord Cornford regained his health and spirits
to a degree where even the faithful Suddaby began
to lapse in his attendance until he was coming up to
see him only twice a week.

That was not the only cause of my lord's satisfaction: for, now that he was up and about again, he
found that he could look out from any window of the
house without risk of the disagreeable sight of his
heir riding busily about the place; and he could
inspect the vague outline of the Dower House through
the trees and be conscious that, for the first time in
two decades, Sarah, Marchioness of Cornford, was
not ensconced within its walls, but miles away,
exerting herself strenuously upon the task of prepar-
ing the Mount Street mansion for its first London
season in an age; a task which, for all my lord's
masculine ignorance of such undertakings, he feared
must be very tiring work indeed for anyone after
such a long period of disuse. And not only was the
boy there with her, lending her a little present-day
bronze which (he felt vaguely) his mam might stand
a shade in need of, but Philippa, too, was removed
from under his feet.

He doubted, privately, whether the Dowager would achieve a success in that particular quarter where his wife's sister had repeatedly failed, but at least Pippy's jewels were already paid for; and the still-rankling cost of them made him reluctant to accept finally that their continued display must not turn the trick in the end.

A more immediate benefit to be derived from her absence from Hoadoak was that he could issue internal orders once again, without the well-meaning chit interpreting them for him all the time. He was very happy with the temporary elevation of Mrs Boon to Philippa's dignities within his establishment. And, finally, he was glad that no giggling younger female voices now disturbed his hours of recuperating tranquillity in his bookroom—even if the price to be found for that was a couple of Court-dresses, and a whole host more sparklers. Although he had managed to hold out against his mother's blithe proposal to send him a Dutch reckoning for the whole, without particulars, he had not demurred that his family were to be rigged out in the first style of elegance while in London, together with the refurbished mansion. As long as mam saw to it (he had told her) that the boy betted no more than was genteel, it would all be paid for *within reason*.

The departure of those bound for Mount Street had comprised an imposing cavalcade, led by the Dowager's own chaise. That venerable equipage, which had been unearthed from a barn and toiled upon for a week by two blacksmiths and a wheelwright, before it was pronounced road-worthy, had two suitably crusty-looking grooms riding beside it. The Ladies Ellen and Margaret accompanied their grandmama inside. There followed the much more modest coach containing Humphrey and his elder

sister, and behind that two further vehicles carrying
a half-smothered Miss Chance and Mr Grimes, and
an assortment of trunks and portmanteaux from
both the Hoadoak houses; by far the majority of such
contents having come from the smaller one, as
Philippa's rather set expression reflected as they
jogged along. Bringing up the rear was a lumbering
fourgon, also dating from the Dowager's heyday,
which was crammed with various maids and movables
and also transported Mr Leach, the cook whose
talents were so wasted in the country and whom
the Dowager had shrewdly prised away from her
son for the duration of the Season.

But my lord had jibbed in no uncertain manner at
the attempted removal of his butler; and this the old
lady recalled with a pursed red lip when her carriage halted at last, and she peered up with alert
attention to the entrance to Cornford House.

She noticed first that the knocker was still tied.
Framed in the doorway stood a portly, glossy
individual—every inch of him the hired town servant
—flanked by two footmen in dark, undistinguished
livery and wearing their own unpowdered hair, she
saw with severity. Emitting a dour snort, she stiffly
alighted and advanced upon the welcoming entourage.

"My lady—" the butler began in sonorous accents,
but she silenced him with a daunting "*Hrrmph!*"
and passed inside.

Once she was inside the hall, however, her grim
expression changed perceptibly. The sight of the
dull, dusty chandelier overhead, the glimpse through
open doors of faded wallpapers and chairs in holland
covers, exercised a markedly different effect upon
her than the predominant one which struck her
grandchildren as they joined her.

Humphrey was the first to comment, in typically

forthright tones. "Good God, ma'am! And how shall *this* be brought up to the nines in time, eh?"

Lady Margaret, hard upon his heels and with her dark eyes looking everywhere, sniffed her pretty nose and announced that it was now fairly plain why Papa had not cared a rush whether the mouldy old place was opened or not. Lady Ellen, already blundering in all directions like an inquisitive pup, squealed invisibly from one room: "Meggy!—come here, pray! Oh, what a *gigantic* ballroom! We shall be able to have all the ton in here, twice over, without the teeniest squeeze!"

"Then it will not serve," replied the seemingly unimpressionable twin she had addressed, going to join Ellen with an air of studied languor; though her eyes were very wide and shining. "For everyone knows that a ton party has not the slightest chance of succeeding unless it *is* a squeeze, slow-top!"

The Dowager had nothing to say to any of this chatter. Perhaps she did not hear it, so rapt and remote was her face as she looked once again upon her old home. And Philippa too (though for different reasons) was left bereft of speech when she stepped beside the old lady and gazed anxiously around. Then she burst forth: "Oh *no*! We shall *never in a thousand years* have it got ready in time! I had *no notion* it was so run-down—else I should *never* have consented to place myself at this stand!"

For the first time, her confident brother now seemed inclined to share some of her apprehensions over his scheme. He put up his glass and strode falteringly up and down the length of the hall, examining various objects through the lens and uttering faint sounds of dismay over most of them. His spirits were lowered further by seeing not one glimpse of Italianate marble on the wholly wooden great stairs.

"Oh, you wouldn't, gel, wouldn't you?" the Dowager grunted suddenly, making Philippa start. "But then you don't know it as I do . . . Fetch that rascal to me who met us outside! Ah, you, man!—is a female yet engaged to hold household? If so, have her attend me in ten minutes in the Green Saloon—that's in there, if ye don't know it yet!" And with a terse nod of her towering head she hobbled away into another large room off the hall, her heels clattering as noisily as a man's boots over the uncovered floors.

After the apparition from the past had disappeared from view, with an air of constraint the butler said: "I am Hubbard, my lord: and that, I collect, was your mother, the, er, late marchioness? And you, madam, would be the present Lady Cornford?"

"God no!—just m'sister!" Humphrey told him distractedly. "And m'grandmother ain't quite 'late' yet awhile, eh, Pip?" At which witticism he gave a nervous crack of laughter, to hide how perturbed and disappointed he in fact was to find the House so lamentably beneath his expectations. For in addition to those they had brought up with them, several servants had gone ahead from Hoadoak a week before. Together with the agency contingent they had comprised a sufficient force of preparers to give the place a deal more polish than this, he felt aggrievedly. He was persuaded that it was precisely the kind of thing which would be avoided if Italian servants were engaged.

He raised his glass once again, this time to peer disconsolately at a bust of the Fourth Marquis; but soon perceived that the poor fellow (like the patch of ceiling above him) had been severely rained upon at some stage, so that where his right eye was moulded the orb had lost definition, lending the bust a grotesque winking effect. With a sigh of defeat he tucked the glass away and gazed bleakly in front of him, with only the strength of his own unaided vision focused upon a bare and peeling wall.

It only remained for Miss Chance to enter, and depress his and Philippa's spirits still more. And, when that morose lady's maid did appear, formally in the lead of the other newly-arrived servants, her response was exactly what Philippa would have expected from her. Her countenance became more bracket-faced still, her eyes smouldered with yet more imaginary hurts and resentments, and she beckoned to the footman staggering behind with her baggage and enjoined him: "Take my—my few belongings directly to my chamber—I assume there is an inhabitable chamber set aside for me?—and *pray do not touch the walls with it along the way,* lest the wet-rot should penetrate my—my humble possessions . . ."

"I knew I should not have brought her!" Philippa declared heatedly when Miss Chance had gone upstairs. "But Papa is so obstinate over small things! Just because the wife of some crony of his commended that human crab-apple, I am forced to suffer her until—as you would say—I give the whole endeavour up and become an ape-leader! Oh, how wishful I am that I had my dear old Alice with me still!"

"You mean you can't turn her off?" murmured Humphrey, intrigued out of his sullens at hearing of such an arrangement. "Seems devilish off."

"Whenever I attempt to do so—which is very often—Papa employs his turn for evasiveness. I hazard you know what I mean . . ."

"Ah, *that*! Now that I can apprehend, sister," the heir said with feeling. "It is exactly the same when I try to wrest a bit of thatch for a cottage roof out of him."

This comfortable grumbling between the pair of

them continued for a while longer, and had the effect of soothing Philippa's nerves to the point where, upon looking about her more carefully, she began to perceive that the condition of the house was not quite so bad as first appearances had suggested. Her face began to grow less clouded, but then Mr Grimes walked cheerfully into the hall, bringing up the rearguard of the arriving servants and saying in his high voice: "Madam—your lordship—may I enquire of the whereabouts of my mistress?"

"But—you are not supposed to be here!" Philippa cried in unguarded consternation. "Granny *promised me faithfully* that you should not—!" She choked silent, feeling her cheeks firing up once more.

The spry old footman's answering grin was oily and mocking. "Ah, but you see she can't do without *me*, m'lady," he said with assured complacency.

Philippa fought for composure and set her jaw, eyeing her grandmother's quaint follower in a way that made a watchful look come into even his expression of brazen confidence. She said very softly: "Proceed first to your chamber. I myself—depend on it—will straightway acquaint your mistress with the fact of your arrival."

When Grimes had bowed his deep old-fashioned bow and trotted off, Humphrey, faintly conscious of the renewed ire seething in his sister's breast, remarked: "That's a devilish rum footman she's got there, ain't it, Pip? A shade old and bishoped for me own taste! Y'know, I found when I was in—"

But before he could impart to her the fascinating intelligence that the best Genovese families never retained their footmen beyond the first bloom of youth, he realised to his surprise that she was no longer with him, but had crossed the hall and was banging the door of the Green Saloon, with quite unnecessary force, behind her. "Devilish rum," he repeated to himself; though this time the sentiment was applied more to feminine caprice in general than to the peculiarities of his grandmother's man-servant.

The old lady's back was turned to the door when Philippa entered, and she was looking out through the tall sash window with the same dreaming airs which she had earlier displayed in the hall. But Philippa was now in no mood to humour this touching nostalgia any longer. "Grandmama—I see that Grimes is here," she said in ominous tones. "And you are perfectly aware we agreed he should remain behind in Kent!"

"What, dear? Speak up, you are on my bad side," the Dowager countered skilfully, moving away from the window with a sweet smile upon her face, and brushing against a small pier table placed against the wall there. Idly pulling aside its covering, and displaying some attractive ormolu and ebony, she mused: "Ah—I was used to put my letters here—alas, so long ago . . ."

"Granny, not to change the subject *if you please.*"

"Very good, dear, there is no cause to raise your voice. I find I can hear you well enough, now I am turned about the right way to you," said Sarah Freen, with the plaintive meekness that had cozened so many of the stronger sex when she was Philippa's age. But her old eyes were swiftly registering the fact that such simple ploys would not serve her now with the jobating chit before her. She suddenly reverted to her usual rasp: "That top-lofty dresser of yours won't pass, my gel."

Philippa had opened her mouth to object—more sternly still—to prevarications of this nature; but then, observing something inscrutable in the masklike painted face across the room, she responded uncertainly: "Oh, and why do you say that, Granny?"

"Pooh, they're plain enough, that species! Sour-phizzed, disobligin', won't do this, shan't care for that, can't like anything . . . She was Cornford's doltish choice, never yours."

The old lady was eyeing Philippa now with a teasing expression which, she suddenly realised, was uncannily like Grimes's out in the hall just now. The pair of them, in spite of the disparity in birth and other obvious differences, were in some respects very alike; just as two people often did seem to grow alike after they had lived—But she put that particular reflection hurriedly aside, sending her aged relation a darkling look tinged with grudging respect.

"Granny, you overheard Miss Chance and Humph and myself out in the hall! In fact, you hear extremely well, whichever of your 'sides' anybody should happen to be on—when it suits you to!" she accused with a faint smile.

Sarah Freen shrugged her man-ish shoulders and said: "Fanciful gel! Now—I say we shall get rid of that dresser of yours before she settles in. I shall attend to that matter myself—a creature like that could well rip up at you and leave you all in a twang for days, just when you need to watch your looks. While as for that rascal of mine," she added casually, "I dare swear you'll—"

"Ah yes, Mr. Grimes!" Philippa interjected, pinching her lips together as she saw how it was to be. "I suspicioned we should roundabout back to him in the end! He, dear grandmama, in exchange for your kind services between me and Miss Chance, is to remain here at Mount Street, I collect?"

"Oh, I think so, child, don't you? I know I said before that he should stay behind in the country—but he has such a roaming eye, you know. I bethought me it would be best to fetch the rascal to-town with us."

"A *roaming eye? Mr Grimes?*" Philippa could not help herself saying at this juncture. She now regarded her grandmother with something very like awe. "*Really!*" she expostulated beneath her breath, feeling the burn in her cheeks.

This spontaneous remark (heard perfectly, it seemed) earned her a baleful glare, and the almost shouted reproof: "Don't you throw your shabby-genteel moralities in *my* teeth, miss! *You*, who we see can't hold on to a man for *two dances* shall not patronise *me* who's been dangled after by so many fine catches that I lost count before I was half your age! Be off with you!—and send in Miss Whatever-she's-called as soon as I've instructed the house-keeper."

"Chance, Granny," said Philippa, now feeling an urge to laugh at her relation's empurpled visage, although she was still shocked by this outrageous confirmation of her long-harboured suspicions.

"Mischance ... aye, she'll think it was, I'll be bound, the day she crossed me," Sarah Freen punned grimly.

Indeed it was almost with a sense of regret that Philippa presently despatched a footman to her haughty dresser with a message that the old lady was waiting upon her downstairs; a feeling that was increased when Miss Chance came stepping crossly down and went into the Green Saloon.

After a few moments, two voices were raised at each other within its confines; then only the Dowager's was audible, in a quiet and crushing mono-logue. And then Miss Chance emerged.

At least, she *slightly resembled* Miss Chance, as

Philippa caught a fleeting glimpse of her through the door of the music-room, where she was then standing; but the figure in the hall looked and held herself like someone she had really never seen before. Quite gone was the lofty demeanour, the peevish expression; her face was very white and had no expression at all. The dresser proceeded numbly back upstairs to her despised new chamber, re-packed her 'humble belongings', and soon afterwards, terminated her brief sojourn at Cornford House.

Eight

The Dowager's energies were shortly expended on several matters which were of considerably more moment to her than the dismissal of a dresser; and very soon Cornford House began to regain if not the splendours of her former residency (for that, she gave Philippa to understand, was scarcely possible in these times of decay), at least a passable enough elegance to accommodate the ramshackle society which she now resigned herself to seeing there.

She was, in fact, extremely helpful to Philippa in some ways, though as vexatious in others. Her formidable mien obtained preferment from tradespeople and those of conditions alike, where, Philippa knew, her own compliant nature would have achieved far less; but, on the other hand, it was annoying for her to take the girls to Bruton Street, as she did one afternoon in search of what Sarah had described to them as: 'my pet modiste in London'—there to discover that both this lady's personal and business names were almost forgotten in that neighbourhood; or to repair to Conduit Street, on another occasion,

to find: 'that sweet milliner who made my beautiful
head-dress when I supped with Prince Edward'—
only to see that those premises had now fallen into a
sadly less exalted style of ownership, and one which
made her hastily bustle the gaping twins away from
the entrance.

There was also the absurd dénouement over the
matter of a dancing-master. Philippa herself, in the
course of two Seasons, had long since overcome the
intricacies of waltz and quadrille, but since these
necessary steps were rarely danced in Kent, soon
after they were established in town she had applied
to her own teacher in Wardour Street to instruct the
girls; but he was unwell. By then she had learned
the unwisdom of troubling her grandparent in such
difficulties. However, unbeknownst to her, Sarah
had scrawled off a note to a certain gentleman who
(at least in her own permanent view of him) was as
supple and handsome as her two hoydenish younger
charges could possibly deserve or wish for in a
dancing-master.

This gentleman, as it happened, was still extant—
and, when the missive was eventually directed to his
present address in High Holbourn, growing suddenly
weary of his retirement there he made haste into his
old professional toggery, rousted up a musician of
similar vintage and restlessness, and the pair then
enthusiastically boarded a hack for Mount Street.

The bemused-looking jarvey was still waiting outside when Philippa returned in the landaulet from a
shopping expedition. Strange sounds, and high-
pitched shrieks, assailed her ears from within
Cornford House while her equipage was still several
yards from the entrance down the flagway.

Hastening inside, she found half the servants
crowded around the door to the music-room as if to

see a raree-show; and as they melted away to each side of her, she caught a first, unforgettable glimpse through the door of a stout personage in striped stockings and a mothy-looking club wig, twirling himself still with a certain authority, and encircling the waist of a near-hysterical Lady Ellen. Lady Margaret—with a wicked smile—appeared to be practising not so much the waltz itself as the art of casting out lures, to the hard-breathing old fellow with the fiddle. Detecting another sound beside his scraping, Philippa's gaze moved on to the pianoforte —and grimly held there as she registered the seraphically beaming figure of the Dowager: making music with her two contemporaries, for all the world as if the French Revolution was yet to come.

Her familiar admonition: *"Girls! Grandmama!"* had sounded peevish and dispirited even to herself; for she was by now become very weary of her constant role as the oppressive elder sister, who would soon be in her proper place amongst the chaperons. She was sorely tempted, at that particular moment of trial, to wish the mischievous pair well and leave them to Sarah Freen to make what she might of them. But then the various frightening consequences which might follow that irreponsible course of action so alarmed her that she took herself in hand, and coolly thanked and paid-off the perspiring old gentlemen. Whereupon the Dowager began to abuse her roundly from the piano-stool, but she held her own tongue and went upstairs; confining her observations upon this latest maladroit interference to Humphrey when she saw him later, before the old lady herself had come down to the drawing-room.

Of course he only laughed, as she had known he would. "She's full of gig now we're in town, *damme* if she ain't!"

"I don't cavil at her liveliness," she said acidly.
"It's ... oh, it's not her well-meaning attempts to
help that get me on my high ropes, however fated
they are, but things like—well, like the bullion on
all her precious old curtains."

"Eh? Bullion?" said her brother in mystified tones.

"I mean the heavy trimming on them ... awful
gold stuff she so admires. If I had my way I'd—oh,
good evening, Granny! We were just wondering when
you would be down!"

"*Hrrmph!*—and *what* would you do with my fine
old curtains, miss?" said the familiar sturdy figure,
seating herself down solidly on a sofa and wearing
what Philippa saw with dismay was a new old-
fashioned gown, with a jacket bodice, a stomacher,
robings and her usual hoops. She coloured and bit her
lip. "Well, ma'am, to be frank I'd get—"

"Rid of them? *Think*, ninny! My son may be a
booberkin in most ways, but d'you fancy him so
foolish as to pay for new hangings of that quality for
a house this size? Whyever should he, pray, just for
you and them little fatties, eh? ... *Where's that
butler?* I find that town servants, at least, are the
same as ever was—a chuckfarthing set living at
rack and manger—ah, Hubble, there you are!"

"Good evening, my lady," intoned that leading
member of the said chuckfarthing set, with the
stoicism that was now habitual with him where the
Dowager was concerned. "Dinner is now served."

"Thank you, Mr Hubbard," Philippa said to him
with a placating smile. And, leaving her brother to
lend his arm to their outspoken senior, she preceded
them into the dining-room where the girls were
already waiting.

Next morning, as if even she were aware that she
might have gone a little far over the matter of the

antediluvian dancing-master, the Dowager was at her most sensible and incisive when it came to the planning of their own opening dinner and ball.

"Lady Jersey will sit opposite to me here, child, on the sketch I've made here. And Lady Sefton—I knew her mother, a most complete vulgar—one space from her left, for when she tires of civil talk to me and wishes to cose with her friend. Lord Brockhurst is here, with your brother 'twixt him and Lady Curragon. Her girl is *here*—I collect she's butter-toothed, so there's no harm done to our own little fatties from placing her near the light. The twins are best set apart to counter schoolroom whoops, don't you think, dear? One at each end? While as for yourself—" She paused, frowning.

"I am not butter-toothed—merely getting long in them," Philippa said wryly. "Are *my* faults to be concealed or exposed on this occasion?" she asked with more amusement than hurt; for Sarah, in this mood, was at least highly lucid and practical, if somewhat ruthless.

"Don't be so *vastly humble*, all the time, child! No one will shine you down at *this* engagement, you may depend on that!"

"I have no need to, Granny, since I am no longer an eligible."

"Fiddle! I've placed you between Henry Fallon—he addresses himself honourable or some such flummery—and the son of my old friend General Terry. The General was used to be as fat as a flawn, and I hear the boy is just the same. By the by, that reminds me—where did I put that fat Lady Merriman, or Merri-something—for you know it might seem *particular* if one end of the board be all fat together . . . One must know people's weight, dear." And she peered worriedly at the drawing on the paper in

front of her, and at the list of names down one side of
it.

Philippa gave a ripple of laughter. "How did you
acquire all this store of tonnish secrets so soon,
Granny? I declare that Aunt Clem set about the task
very differently!"

"La, if you had been in the real *bon ton* when I
was, a mere trifle of a beginning ball would be
nothing to you! Now, where had we got to—oh yes,
Lady Sarinset goes here, next a very thin young
gentleman named Harris—who is vastly rich but
said to be wary with girls of his own order. So he will
do very well *there*, with just military company on the
other side of him . . . Now we come to Leach's part in
this: can the rascal put up a turbot? I well remember
the wonders he can make from a gobble-cock, but I
always say that *turbot is the test*! You see, child,
your top-lofty cook who loves his main courses will
often liefer have Tommy try his hand at a 'simple
side dish'—only with turbot it don't never fadge!"

Philippa was only half paying attention to her
relative's gossipy drone; she was scanning the list of
names again, her brow furrowed with careful con-
centration. "I cannot like where Humph is placed,
Granny."

"Pooh—it matters not a whit who flanks *him*, only
consider: those silly stocks he wears only let him
face straight in front! I have marked Miss Burrell's
niece as his opposite—and *on the dit* for her says
she's bespoke already despite bein' but sixteen: just
the gel for Master Humphy to talk to of Italy and
Italy and Italy!—eh?"

This total confidence on the part of her mentor
gradually communicated itself to Philippa; and the
occasion itself, including the ball afterwards, passed
off in such smooth style that she was glad the old

lady had had the managing of most of it. Apart from one of the gentlemen seeming a little disguised during a set of quadrilles, and the lamentable performance by the twins of those same scarcely-learned steps, she felt they had made an excellent beginning. The house looked charmingly, the Ladies Jersey and Sefton had been complaisance itself, and she suspected that their kindly amusement over the girls' inept dancing might have served more to procure them Almack's cards than any sheer proficiency would have attained. So, even there, Grandmama appeared to have done good in the end! And it was strange and touching to observe the two celebrated patronesses of the most distinguished club in London both almost toad-eating their eccentric and ancient hostess. When she remembered the icy set-downs that had come the way of poor Aunt Clem, in similar circumstances, Philippa was glad for the first time that her brother had devised his unlikely scheme.

However, although several invitations for the ladies of Cornford House to attend various balls, routs and assemblies arrived during the course of the next week, the precious vouchers were not amongst them; and Philippa sadly concluded that the capricious Lady Jersey had changed her mind.

This setback made but little impression upon the twins, both already having certain *partis* in mind and convinced that they were set fair to become Accredited Toasts without further support. As Lady Margaret confided to Lady Ellen in her practical-minded way, even if the select assemblies were denied them, at least they were incomparably better placed than if their Papa had died, and they were now obliged to languish in the country in black gloves; an opinion with which the warmer-hearted Nell had to concur, if only for Papa's sake.

After the first few engagements, Humphrey began to betray signs of restiveness when it came to requests to squire his sisters about town. He was by then receiving several invitations from hostesses in his own right, and felt—reasonbly enough in his own eyes—that Pippy and the old lady were sufficient company for the two eligibles of the family on most occasions.

One evening in May, when the Season was in full feather, he attended a party in Mayfair thus alone.

At first he expected that it would bore him, for the talk there was all of the Regent being served with some notice from his wife that she desired to return to Kensington Palace. Such parochial *on-dits* were of little interest to the Italianate young nobleman who stood there leaning negligently on the drawing-room mantelpiece, taking an occasional snuff from his Roman box and staring sombrely in front of him at the rather small area of the room which his shirt-points allowed him to survey from that position. Considering that this was fated to be a somewhat momentous evening in his life, it began, as he was later to remark, 'deuced tamely.'

After a while, and with an air of no little complaisance, he stood up for a set of country dances. His first partner was squinny-eyed and talked incessantly of the Regent. Her successor on his arm was much the same. But then—it happened!

"I should be honoured, ma'am, to—" But the rolled-off words withered on his tongue as he groped for his glass, and raised it with a hand that shook slightly.

"Oh my God—it cannot be!" exclaimed his prospective partner, drawing back as if the suggestion that had been put to her were infamous. "But it *is*!" And these startling words were followed by a lusty crack of mirth which drew every ear and eye in the room to them—and took Humphrey painfully back in time to when he had sat in a certain French public coach, with a certain schoolroom miss whose want of conduct he could remember even now.

"*God* . . ." he echoed aghast, letting the glass drop. "How did you get—why did they let—what are you—?"

"Which are the very same sort of questions, my lord, that I am tempted to ask of you in that *dandy rig!*" observed Miss Thouvenal in tremulous accents.

He knew now who it was well enough! Putting him to blush within seconds, just as before! He fought for countenance, saying doggedly: "I—I trust you are well, ma'am, after your own foreign experiences. I would scarcely know you," he added, with his usual forthrightness where feminine acquaintances were concerned.

But Miss Thouvenal, now as previously, seemed too blunt and matter-of-fact herself to notice much of what he said to her beyond the surface meaning. "Oh, in good enough case to out-last the Season, I daresay . . . Did I tell you back in France that we were seeking our father's grave in the Peninsula? Well, we never found it! Mama dragged us over half Spain searching, and secured the patronage of General de Flahaut himself, but it came to naught in the end. Then mama subsided into permanent vapours and it fell to me to bring us all home in one piece . . . Lord Begbroke—I cannot remember you at all as such a magnificent Pink of the Ton when we first met!—pray tell me, what occasioned such a transformation? Your hated Tour? I cannot believe that very easily!"

Her eyes twinkled at him as the fiddlers struck up again, and he drew her towards him in the dance.

They were rather fine eyes, he recalled without enthusiasm; very dark and foreign, like her hair. The latter was no longer curled as he remembered it, but worn smoothly braided into a Quakerish coronet on top, which lent her needed height since she was still quite smallish. Her gown was a slim and simple three-quarter dress of primrose sarsnet, over an underdress of ivory. "Are those real pearls in your ears?" he grunted suspiciously.

She snorted with amusement. "Now, that does sound more in the style of my gallant travelling companion! Are those real diamonds on your shoes, my lord?"

He glowered at her as they moved together, angry to be bested with such ease. Searching for a means of dashing her down, he bethought him of what she had just said and observed with a lofty inflection: "I collect you still mix in 'Imperial' circles, then, ma'am—since you spoke of General de Flahaut. He has politically survived his 'Emperor', so I understand from the *Morning Post*. I am glad to learn that he was of some service to *your* family, at least . . ."

She chuckled appreciatively. "Oh, your trick, my lord! But why so stuffish? It is plain to me that your travelling has indeed changed you vastly, in many ways. Tell me about it—how long have you returned to England?—I should have supposed that you would be abroad still, to take in all the Tour countries—or did Boney's last throw put you in a fever to be home again, as it did so many others?"

Her final words were not spoken in a sharp way, and she took care to refrain from talking of emperors to his bleak visage. Unbending slightly, he told her of his father's illness; to which news (doing the chit justice) she said all that was proper.

Mollified, he found himself putting further questions to her, even though he had just sworn not to. "You look quite modish . . . Are you freshly come-out like my younger sisters, Miss Thouvenal?"

"Yes: I stay with my Aunt Harvey—there she sits now, the one knotting the red shawl—at Hanover Square. On the south side," she added defensively.

"At where?" he queried blankly, though without conscious *hauteur* as he was merely a little bewildered by this answer; Hanover Square was only a vague direction to him, so it seemed unfair of Miss Thouvenal to misunderstand and say so waspishly:

"Aha! We are unfashionably remote from where you and your sisters reside, I collect!—is that why your lip curls, my lord?"

"We are fixed at m'father's house—Mount Street," he said, eying her uncertainly and wondering at her tone.

Conversation between them seemed inclined to falter beyond this point, and he felt an odd blend of disappointment and relief when the set concluded and someone else stepped up to claim her for the waltz. Disturbed, and somehow annoyed, by the encounter, he went to take his leave of the hostess. Outside, in a kind of stupid daze which came from thinking that Miss Thouvenal had remembered meeting him for above two years, he sent John Coachman home by mistake—and was then obliged to go on by hack to the rout at Holland House, where he was also engaged that same evening.

There, too, the vapid talk was all of Court matters. He heard very little of it, his mind floating back continually to the surprise of meeting Miss Thouvenal again. But, after making a sadly inattentive fourth at cards for a time, a neighbouring conversation did gradually draw his interest.

". . . but you've physicked me enough tonight, Guy, and so I say I'll take no more medicine! My mind won't stick to the play, not what with the other *monstrous thing* we spoke of earlier! You asked me then what it signified, beyond a Cheltenham tragedy in print—it signifies *this*, my boy: it signifies that Lady Caroline Lamb ain't up to snuff nor never was! I stand square with those who wish her to Jericho! For only consider: 'tis one thing to write a *plaidoyer* against her husband—which ain't to say that ain't infamous too—but *damme*, to have the gall to rip up at the Duchess of Devonshire!—*and* her ma!—*and* Lady Melbourne!—*and* Sally Fane!—*and* them poor Granvilles! You needs to read some of the stuff twice to set the right cap on each of 'em—but it's no puzzle to see which coxcomb Glenarvon is cast for, since all the world knows *that* devil! Her La'ship can make what cake she likes out of him with my blessing! But *by God*, if *I* had the bridling of that libellous filly for her impudence, I'd break every bone in her!—and a dozen good whips besides!"

None of this violent speech diverted Humphrey overmuch from his cards and counters; but the short drawled reply made both fall from his hands.

"It's cattish, Percy, I grant that, but you can't gainsay its cleverness."

Humphrey slewed his whole body around in his chair; as his collar-points necessitated even at moments of direst emotion such as at present. "*You!*" he muttered thickly.

There were some scandalised sounds from his own cardpartners, and a short pause of astonishment from the two conversing gentlemen at the next table. Then the broad shoulders of the last speaker were slightly turned, and Humphrey found himself once

more face-to-face with Major Hipsley of the Dragoon
Guards.

Anne Thouvenal and her aunt had quit Dover Street
not long after Humphrey, and boarded the job-chaise
and pair which carried them northward.

When that jolting equipage was set in motion,
Mrs Harvey said: "My, what a squeeze! My dear, I
am just not cut out for it at all! I feel so old amongst
the other gooseberries, and tho' I daresay this is only
natural because I *am* old, I find I don't care to have it
rammed down my throat night in and night out!
Who was that tall fair boy in the peculiar clothes,
who stood there like a stock with you in the second
set?" she enquired abruptly at the end of her flow of
complaints.

Anne smiled, shifting her head on the squabbed
seat-back to look with understanding and affection
at her companion. She knew that Mrs Harvey truly
disliked fashionable company, and did not just pre-
tend to in the manner of so many of the women of all
ages who avidly attended the assemblies.

She was a small person like herself, but with her
dead brother's ruddy English complexion and mouse-
coloured hair. Although she was now conscientiously
turned out in purple crape, and with a little Alexan-
drian cap upon her head, she was only really content
when in her village near Spalding, in Lincolnshire;
keeping her chickens from the fox rather than
guarding eligible nieces from men of the town. Anne
was grateful to her for undertaking the exchange of
tasks, in general, so cheerfully. She had launched
two of her sisters last year, and now herself, from
the hired house at Hanover Square; coming up there
each spring with her old butler, and only engaging
London maidservants for the duration of the Season.

"A Lord Begbroke, whom I met when Mama took us on that crazy last journey, Aunt," she said musingly.

"A lord? What breed of a lord?" asked Mrs Harvey, with her rural turn of phrase. Sporting lords she had a certain amount of time for—since they tended to kill fowl-eating foxes—but, in the main, she suspicioned they must be Dangerous; at least when of dancing rather than fence-taking age.

"An Earl: prospectively a Marquis." .

Mrs Harvey began to look thoughtful despite her prejudices. Anne could almost hear her thinking: 'A prospective Marquis . . . renewing an aquaintance with every sign of agitation and flusteredness . . . Perhaps I'm not wasting my time in this hateful city after all . . .'

She gave a gay laugh at Mrs Harvey's confirmative expression, and squeezed her arm. "Don't get up high hopes there!—the wind doesn't sit in that quarter, I assure you! Lord Begbroke is very much too coltish for my taste."

"Coltish? He did not appear so to me—I should have reckoned him a beau of the first whatever-it-is," her relative said vaguely.

"First Stare, Aunt—and how out you would be!"

Mrs Harvey bridled a trifle, not caring to have her countrified ignorance flung in her face even though she was secretly rather proud of it. She said: "That smart's coat, those pale pantaloons—a good figure he has, by the by—and that peculiar glass he kept flourishing at you—how all that makes the poor man coltish, I just cannot apprehend!"

Anne smiled thoughtfully. "Underneath 'all that', he is not so unlike you."

"Like *me*! You must be out in our cock-loft!" cried

the astounded chicken-keeper, careless of the coach-man's ears.

"No, really, Aunt—when I met him first, just after he had shot a dragoon in a duel, he was the most blockish and countrylike thing you ever saw! Rather sweet, also," she added hastily; but then coloured and bit her lip at Mrs Harvey's expression. She continued in a raised voice: "And I find him *exactly the same now*, beneath all his absurd new foppery! Oh, he is just another regular young buck home from the Tour, and fancying himself steeped in ancient culture! They say that some men never grow up, however hard they may try, and he is the living proof of that theory, the bandbox creature! *I* do not intend to figure as his latest flirt, be he never so much a lord!"

Mrs Harvey preserved a thoughtful silence for the remainder of their journey home. At first, her mind was full of fright at the reference to duels and shooting which had dropped so casually from her niece's lips. But when she had reasoned such fears away, with the reflection that it was doubtless just an example of the Earl's bamming talk to a girl he was taken with (an explanation which generally pleased her), she began to ponder, as she often pondered all sorts of different matters, in terms of her absent and much-missed poultry yard back in Lincolnshire.

Although she was a parson's widow of adequate means, Mrs Harvey had made quite a name for herself in chicken-keeping circles that extended far beyond her home county. She had been conscious of a certain flair for poultry since early girlhood, and more recently had even originated a special breed of fowl, known far and wide as the Spalding Blue. Much of her hostility towards the London Season was governed by the latter's awkward coinciding with the time of year when, by rights, she should have been setting eggs, and supervising broody hens, instead of leaving these crucial duties for others to attend to during her frivolous absence.

However, she was now recalling that some of the very best and most successful matches which she had contrived in her yard had begun with a great show of contemptuous disdain on the part of a selected pullet: the cockerel's view of the affair was generally unimportant, she had learned, but a too-complaisant hen bird was never a good sign; she always terminated such false promise instantly, and tried the mis-mated birds with others whom they swore at.

"I daresay you know best, dear," she said equably as the chaise rolled into the Square.

Nine

But for Major Hipsley's deep and distinctive voice,
probably the two ex-duellists would not have known
each other after such a long interval.

For the Major was no longer resplendent in the
uniform of a cavalry officer, though his companion
at the card table wore full regimentals. And as for
Humphrey, the Major's chilly but puzzled expression
made it clear that he saw no resemblance at all
between this fiery-faced exquisite before him now
and the greenhead who had shot him down, with
such stupendous dishonour, at Johnson's Clearing in
Stelling Minnis, two years ago.

He stood up, rather stiffly, from his chair and said:
"Was that to my address? Who are you, sir? In any
event, I think you are not known to me . . ."

He concluded these few words with an ironic half-
shrug of his powerful frame under the coat of black
superfine which was moulded to it. One fob only
hung at his waist, and his blunt hands were innocent of jewellery. He wore none at all bar a single
stone which scarcely showed beneath the folds of his

neck-cloth. His dark pantaloons merged with dress shoes of Spanish leather. Altogether, a more marked contrast between his own sober appearance, and that of the person who was excitably confronting him, could not have been made had it been contrived.

Humphrey's bottled-up fury suddenly overflowed, as he rose to his feet and felt Hipsley's contemptuous hard stare raking up and down him. He burst forth: "Aye, it was! For solely because of you and your *curst reputation*, I have had to stay abroad for *two whole years*!—with pockets to let, moreover, since I was at outs with my father—*again because of you*!—and with that lobcock of a chaplain set upon my back, for every mile of ground we rolled over—in *foreign public coaches*! *And all because of you*!"

Guy Hipsley's stern and rather heavy features had been slowly altering during this crescendo of reproaches. "Good God! Lord Begbroke!" he now ejaculated. "All ten foot of you! Well, I'll be damned!"

It was now the turn of the Major's friend to regard Humphrey with a pair of light blue eyes that distinctly lacked warmth in his round and pleasant face. "Lord *Begbroke*, Guy, eh?" he murmured in discreet but hostile accents. "I take it this is the feller who—?" His voice tailed off into a speaking glance at Hipsley.

The latter gentleman unexpectedly laughed. (And Humphrey started backward, as though that laugh were a palpable slap in his face.) "To be sure it is! My vanquisher himself! The one man to bring it off in four engagements!—and the one who fetched me down on earth in more ways than one! My lord, I have waited a deuce of a long time for this moment, and to shake hands with you!"

And, in apparent accord with this extraordinary statement, the Major stepped forward—with rather a pronounced limp—holding his large right hand affably extended.

Humphrey found himself touching fingers by polite instinct; then shrank back as if Hipsley had the smallpox. He spluttered furiously: "You have a turn for satire, sir . . . as well as one for ruining lives wheresoever you go!"

Guy Hipsley now looked a trifle pained as he withdrew the hand of friendship and thoughtfully stroked his upper lip with it. "Now look you here, m'lord," he began quietly, "I'll—"

"No, sir! You'll pitch *no more of this gammon to me!*" Humphrey brayed, now thoroughly overset by this strange development of a scene which he had often mentally rehearsed, but never remotely imagined as taking this form. He waved his arms at the Major in a manner that seemed eloquent of contempt and disdain to himself; but appeared somewhat doltish to the several interested eyes that were now focused upon the pair of them.

But then he spoiled the grand spurning gesture, even in his own estimation, by grunting spontaneously: "What d'you mean, in *four* engagements? Are you a liar on top of the rest, sir? For all the world knows you have killed nine men!"

The Major's mouth had slightly compressed when the word liar was used; now, though, he recomposed his features and laughed his calm deep laugh once more, saying: "The world, my lord, is inclinded to do it rather too brown when it recounts such affairs: I assure you that is true in my own case."

His auditor gaped at him, then blustered: "Damn your impudence! D'you think me a halfling?"

"No: tho' perhaps something of slow-top."

Since being insulted afresh, Hipsley's face had now almost reverted to its former dour stiffness. It was an arresting face, as even his fulminating ex-adversary reflected for a second or two, amidst the white-heat of his baffled rage. When the man smiled he was almost handsome, with the dark slanted brows seeming somehow to join in with the movement of the full and sculptured lips. But when he ceased to smile, as at present, he looked exactly like the devil he remembered in the half-light at Johnson's Clearing.

Before Humphrey could draw more breath to utter further insults, Hipsley suddenly laid those two sizable hands of his upon both of his own heaving shoulders, pressing him down firmly into his seat once more. Kicking his own chair around to face him, in the negligent manner of an officer who was accustomed to applying his boot to mess furniture, he sat down himself again and said in a quiet but tenacious way: "Now, may *I* put an oar in, my lord? Apprehend this, if you please! I, too, could prate and whine over the outcome of our rendezvous if I allowed myself! The scandal of it ran on . . . alarmingly after you scored such an, er, signal victory over me that time. Indeed, it ran to a point where I deemed it right—or, at least, prudent—to sell out: Captain Webster here will confirm that if you doubt my word. And if you are now wondering whether I had a fortune tucked by to fall back on—how glaringly out you are, Lord Begbroke, I regret to tell you! When I resigned, I had little more than my colours and four hundred guineas: and nigh the whole of that sum was betted and lost down the maw of Tatt's inside a month! And in case you are forgetting, my lord—I also had a brace of near-useless legs into the bargain!"

Throughout most of this speech Humphrey had been attempting to interrupt with the observation that it was by far the most brummish tale he had heard in his life; by the end of it, however, his commonsense had prevailed sufficiently over his passions for him to take note of the unmistakable ring of honesty in the Major's voice. If the man were acting, then he was another Kean. "Only four hundred, eh?" he grunted, much struck. For even he himself, during his worst times of impecunious banishment, had been breeched far more serviceably than his antagonist.

That faint stirring of sympathy led him to phrase his next question in more civil terms than he would else have employed. "I collect you were forever craving to—to kill me, once your legs were mended?"

Hipsley simply chuckled by way of answering this fell speculation; which had occasioned shame and exile on the one hand, and an equal shame together with the loss of a career upon the other. His meaning was clear enough, but he said seriously: "Oh, I won't deny that for a day or two I thought of doing what my colonel feared I should: burn you to death with powder-flare some dark night!—or hire some millers from Gentleman Jackson's to pound you to a pulp! But no, lad: not once I had thought the thing through. You fetched me up short when I had grown to regard nobody's opinion of my temper and my actions but my own. I should never, never have picked on a young—" He coughed and continued: "—should never have picked on a man who was as castaway as you." He gave a thoughtful sigh. "There's naught like pain to lesson a fool, don't they say?—and by God, *I had pain!* I still get a little, from the offside limb." He slapped the latter tenderly, then grinned and added: "But t'other's as good as new now—I mean the one you *didn't* ball from under me, but merely bounced me on in that tavern!"

The round-faced man in the dress uniform had been observing this exchange for some moments with a more relaxed mien. He now deftly interposed: "Guy, what say the three of us make a night of it, eh? His lordship here looks to me like a man who's had his fill of polite society for one night—and I know you have, you old devil! And consider, Guy, before you jump down my throat, that nothing would now serve your reputation better than being seen arm-in-armly with the one you called out so cheap! While as for you, my lord—I'd vouch that no medicine could ease your bile half so well as finding out for yourself that Guy ain't the murderous scaff you take him for! Now, both of you—what d'you say?"

In fact both gentlemen were equally taken aback by the Captain's bland appeal to them; both hastily opened their mouths to be held excused; and both slowly closed them again as each realised that he did not wish to be the one to cry it down.

Captain Webster observed them with a half-smile playing about his shrewd rotund countenance. "Come, now, my game-cocks! A few drinks together don't mean getting leg-shackled! I appeal to the same sense of honour which brought you to pistols in the first place!" he added infuriatingly.

"Er, I thank you but—I don't drink any more—not since—you know—at least, except for the Italian wind . . ." Humphrey said at last.

"Italian wine?" Guy Hipsley repeated blankly. "What the deuce do you swill that stuff for?"

This crude assault upon Latin culture set matters back a trifle between them, until the Captain contrived to smooth them down again. And so it shortly afterwards came about that a flabbergasted Humphrey (at first very much on his high ropes) accompanied the man who was his greatest enemy to various well-known establishments in west London which catered, more or less exclusively, for gentlemen who were desirous of sampling the pleasures of the town free from feminine supervision and encumbrance.

Next day, not much of what had passed during the hectic hours of darkness was very clear to Humphrey, as he cautiously discussed a small nuncheon of toast and preserves at Mount Street. But he had learned, during the course of their increasingly enjoyable carouse, that Peter Webster (as that conciliatory officer was now known to him) had somehow been responsible—naturally it had only been hinted—for repairing the Marjor's fortunes at the time of their lowest ebb after he had quit the Guards.

And the good Captain Webster appeared to have achieved a further success in his latest endeavours to rehabilitate his friend; for Humphrey, despite the temporary uncertain state of his head, was now strongly of the opinion that the whole sad business of his duel with Hipsley had been no more than a wretched hum. For the undeniable truth was, the Major was a bang-up fellow—perhaps one who was a shade lacking in ton, and obviously no ladies' man with his rough ways, but no less of a Goer for that. He now had not the least objection in the world to making his acquaintaince again, should that occasion arise while both of them were in London.

That proposal had been aired in more definite terms by the Captain, just before the merry trio parted company in the early morning; but although it was greeted with loud cries of assent from each of the ex-duellists, nothing had actually been arranged between them for a further meeting; an omission which the Captain had thought disappointing, but had been unable to overbear as before, since his persuasive tongue was somewhat thickened by that stage.

Lady Philippa, too, was feeling at her best that day.

As evening approached, and she once again sat wearily at her dressing-table, it occurred to her that while the recent Battle of Waterloo had, no doubt, been a very arduous and sanguinary affair for the men who took part in it, in some respects at least the prolonged campaign of the London Season did not lag far behind it for the combative females. She smiled slightly at her reflection in the glass as she pursued the comparison further: in some ways the Season was surely worse than Waterloo—for even the soldiers of Napoleon and Wellington had not fought one another night after night once battle was joined; also they had not had to depend upon the whims and favours of others in order to procure a victory; and they were not hampered by their aged relatives once they were at each other's throats . . .

She beckoned in the mirror to the friendly and obliging abigail who had replaced Miss Chance in her service, but when the girl approached, said to her uncertainly: "Oh, Lord—*I* don't know, Elsie! It is the Opera tonight . . . I suppose my Mama's tiara should be aired—since we go on to a dress-party—but it makes my poor head so ache! Yes, with the lace veil to soften it—and the French kid gloves—and the lilac gauze over my strong rose underdress: you would be amazed to see how that shade shall set off the lilac, Elsie, in a starkly lit-up place such as the Opera-house has become."

Her mind returned fretfully to more intractable problems as the abigail began on her hair.

The twins were not behaving quite as they ought; they seemed to find the whole undertaking a great lark, and little more. Of course, it was only their first London fling, and they were too young to be thinking yet of finding eligible *partis* for themselves, rather than the silly sprigs of fashion they favoured presently; but even so she was disquieted by the schoolroom levity which Ellen, in particular, seemed disposed to bring to all her engagements with the other sex. Margaret's funning took a different turn—and one which her elder sister regarded with less tolerance than Ellen's: she was forever casting out lures to all her partners (even the eldest) in a highly stylised manner which at first merely bewildered them, and then—in one or two regrettable instances—had led them to form conclusions which that young lady's only budding poise had not quite been able to contend with unassisted. Indeed, her own hasty interventions had not every time served to rescue Meg from these self-provoked *contretemps* without causing embarrassment to all concerned—except for the young miss herself. She was incorrigibly mischievous; and Philippa had more than once been cross and resentful that their brother was not gallanting the three of them as regularly as he had promised to. Both the girls adored him, and thought his foreign ways tonnish in the extreme; she was convinced they would make a far more determined push to behave themselves if they were more under his eye. Tonight, at least, he had to be with them for the Opera, as she had made clear to him.

Then there was Grandmama ... The old lady's assistance was proving to be somewhat erratic. There were times (as before their opening ball) when her aid had been considerable. But as for her much-vaunted grip upon Society—that was proving to be a doubtful boon, as Philippa had always thought it would. True, it was thanks to her that they were

using the Duke of Devonshire's box tonight at the
Opera: the acknowledged leaders of the ton were
scrupulously attentive to Sarah herself (partly, as
Philippa knew, because eccentrics were all the rage
this year), but her robust attempts to procure their
favours on behalf of her young relatives did not
appear to be bearing much fruit. Almack's opening
night was now long gone, and still no vouchers had
arrived at Cornford House. Soon the girls would be
presented—and how then would the erstwhile 'Queen
of Carlisle's Club' conduct herself? Would she don
the same dyed feathers which had once captivated
Prince Edward, and affix her terrible mouse-skin
eyebrows which had convulsed the entire company
the other evening at Mrs Wellesley Pole's? Even the
Regent had raised his own jaundiced brows at the
sight of them, and creaked forward to bestow a
satirical kiss upon the old lady's hand.

Then, of course, there was her own newly-repeated
failure to fix an eligible interest. She had an uneasy
impression that her face was now become far too
well-known at the various gatherings; people there
tended to greet her with bored smiles, while their
eyes moved on elsewhere; more and more she found
herself gravitating naturally towards the groups of
chaperons—not merely between the dances, as had
happened sometimes last year, but now, quite often,
during them also; a significant development of which
she was only too aware.

Ah, well! she told herself, adjusting the nowadays
quite suitable heavy tiara to a more bearable bal-
ance upon her head, and carefully hoisting it aloft as
she stood up, *I am doing my best!—and if I am
saddled with frivolous sisters, an indifferent brother,
that infernal old woman, and myself a born ape-*

*leader—well, then, at least Papa was apprised be-
forehand of all these obstacles to success!*

And still in that defiant mood, she shortly set
forth for the Opera-house.

At about the same time another lady was taking a
realistic stock of her affairs, though in a different
and less fashionable part of town.

Hanover Square had not always been unfashionable; once it had seen gay and famous parties such
as those under the roof of Lord Hillsborough, where
masked gentlemen of the first consequence had
supped with masked ladies of no consequence at
all—but that was now long ago. The Square was
grown both respectable and dull, and was largely let
out, at this time of year, to shabby-genteel match-
makers up from the country, such as Mrs Harvey
from Lincolnshire.

She and her latest ward were unengaged that
evening, after earlier attending a *déjeuné dinatoire*
at Chiswick for the Duke and Duchess of Cumberland.
They had been present with about thirty others,
including the Prince and Princess Esterhazy; and
Mrs Harvey had not scrupled to avail herself of the
chance to wheedle Almack's cards on behalf of her
niece from the elegant wife of the Austrian Ambas-
sador. These attempts had not been well received: in
the end she had been given a crushing set-down, not
that it had troubled that self-possessed rural lady
one whit, but neither had it added to her ward's
enjoyment of the occasion.

That young lady said now: "Aunt: would you not
agree that the sole advantage we have both obtained
from that absurd mid-day dinner is a capacity to go
without food for at least a week?"

Mrs Harvey made no answer, and even Anne was

too tactful to voice her further thought that the *dinatoire* represented about the full extent of her relative's paltry influence in London.

However, Mrs Harvey was perfectly well aware what she was thinking. As they sat cosily together in the drawing-room, thankful at least for a night's respite from the exigencies of the town, and having extended that welcome relief to the servants, she felt sorry for the girl—cross-bred as she was, and possessed of perhaps too strong a character to fix the interest of niminy-piminy townsmen (as she privately regarded most of the beaux who had stood up with Anne at the functions).

The countrified chaperon herself, though she might be hen-minded, was by no means hen-witted or lacking in rumgumption. And since there was not much else for her to do that evening, she applied her mind afresh to the task of doing her best by Anne.

On sudden impulse, she went to a drawer and returned with a set of the rules for Almack's Club, which she had first obtained and studied when attempting to fire off one of Anne's half-sisters, two years before. Seating herself at her desk, and taking up a pencil, she looked again at the listed names of the Patronesses.

The Princess Esterhazy's was there: Mrs Harvey scored it through with some violence. So was Lady Jersey's: her pencil struck another line. There remained the illustrious names of the Ladies Castlereagh, Cowper and Sefton, and that of the Countess Lieven.

Mrs Harvey's pencil summarily dismissed them one by one—until it hovered over Lady Sefton; and then the reason came to her why some vague instinct had sent her looking for the list.

Several years ago, at the time when she was first

introducing the Spalding Blue to an appreciative public, a consignment of that most excellent breed of fowls (or was it just hatching eggs?) had been despatched by her to the country residence of some-one named Sefton. At the time—when she would have been immersed in important matters about her little farm—she had paid only scant heed to the imposing seal upon the letter enquiring about the Blues; and which was repeated on a later missive, thanking her for the stock she had sent and expressing great satisfaction with them.

She hurried to find her order-book, which was luckily with her in London, turning back its pages to find the entry. And there it was!—for two sittings of the Spalding Blue, which had been posted into Nottinghamshire (she now remembered) by the kind offices of a gentleman who was travelling in that direction; and which happy coincidence—thus avoiding the knocks of normal transit—was almost certainly the prime reason why Lady Maria Sefton had been so fortunate as to hatch as many as twenty-five, and rear twenty-three, 'adorable blue chicks'—as her ladyship's last letter, folded with the other in that page of the order-book, disclosed once again to Mrs Harvey's interested eyes.

"Now, I just *wonder*. . ." the chicken-keeper mused to herself in her flat Lincolnshire accent. Ignoring her niece's enquiring glance—for there was no sense in raising her hopes, only, perhaps, for it all to come to fiddlesticks end—she remained at the desk, took up a home-grown quill, dipped it in the standish, and began composing a letter which was addressed to Almack's Club in King Street and opened with the effusive words: *'My Dst. Lady Sefton—'*

Ten

*Humphrey's attention had repeatedly wandered from
the stage throughout the family's visit to the Opera.*

Various reasons accounted for his lack of concen-
tration: he had little natural ear for singing, he was
persuaded that once one had been in Milan there
was nothing else worth hearing, and besides, he had
lost the thread of *Alceste*, soon after its commence-
ment, because of an intrusion into their box by a
drunken courtesan and her escort; his services had
been urgently required by Philippa to put the couple
out, and direct them to the boxes above.

Then there was his extraordinary meeting with
Major Hipsley to mull over, and the Opera afforded
him about the first chance to do so in a state of full
sobriety.

The comradeship of the night before seemed now
to have slightly lost its lustre, though he still wished
Hipsley well enough and was glad that the tawdry
affair was put behind them both for good; and he felt
obliged to the repentant duellist's brother-officer for
mending matters between them so tactfully. They

were both bang-up fellows—though he could not
help owning to the stray thought that it might not
be quite comfortable to meet either of them again.

But it was Miss Thouvenal who mainly occupied
his mind, as the figures sang and gesticulated beneath his unseeing gaze and deaf ears.

. . . Something still rankled with him about that
brief conversation he had had with her at Dover
Street; something he could not pin down, though it
was a quality which he associated with her from the
time of their first acquaintance abroad.

Little by little he began to perceive what lay at
the heart of this feeling. It was her sheer, preposterous *condescension* towards him! *She!*—who, as anyone could tell, lacked a feather to fly with, was
deplorably ramshackle, and, on top of everything,
half-Froggish!

He tried to probe more deeply still why she so
vexed him, and soon tracked it down that the cause
was not so much her original ill-concealed amusement at his plight, but the insufferable way she had
persisted in that attitude towards him only yester-
day; when, if she had eyes in her head, she could
scarcely have failed to discern that he was now a
different being altogether from the Johnny Raw who
had journeyed with her to Paris. Yet she had adopted
precisely the same manner to him as that other
time—as if the Tour, and all the foreign bronze that
it had lent him, had simply never happened.

The flush of resentment in his breast now began to
exceed the very warm atmosphere which pervaded
the Opera-house. *How dare she!* It was the outside of
enough that a girl like that, with no rank and
fashion, should be permitted to move in polite circles; the kind of thing which would never be tolerated in Italy for one second—only in the rum kind of

society which he saw about him now in London. He was dashed if his Granny there (nodding half-asleep against the side of the box, with her feathers a-droop) wasn't in the right of it when she raked London down so: a dab of a girl like Anne Thouvenal being received in Dover Street was living proof of what the old woman said . . .

He fell to brooding morosely just how Miss Thouvenal would have been snubbed in the Continental society he so admired; and then a smile gradually loosened his lips as The Idea first seized hold of his imagination.

A capital idea indeed! God, but *that* would instruct her! Of course, high sticklers might contend that one shouldn't employ such a means unless one's feelings were seriously engaged . . . but where was the harm done, since the chit had no consequence? He soon dismissed such faint scruples, telling himself grimly that Miss T had asked him more than once for a set-down of massive proportions—and now he would do his very best to oblige her!

His vengeful smile faded a little as he perceived that he would require an assistant to bring the thing off in the correct foreign style; but he soon brightened again, remembering that the very man was close at hand. For only a sennight back, in Bond Street, he had recognised amongst the strutters there his old Kentish friend Dick Masterson—the same Masterson who had seconded him at Stelling Minnis, now fixed in town with his mam and sister at Ten, Clarges Street, he fancied his friend had told him. He would see Dick about it tomorrow, first thing!

And indeed he repaired to Clarges Street while Richard was still breakfasting upstairs. Accepting some coffee, Humphrey walked about the room with

it, launching at once into his scheme and waving the
cup to emphasise its main points.

Strangely enough, at first Dick Masterson didn't
appear to grasp how capital it was. Sounding
distinctly doubtful, he grunted: "But *damme*, Humph,
I don't like the sound of—"

"Let me finish! Pray remember, it needn't take
you above five minutes from when you first knock on
their door."

"But, *damme*, I don't know their door!—do you?"
said Masterson, who was now tensely chewing his
toast and looking very unhappy.

"I collect they are on the south side of Hanover
Square. You know, North Village somewhere."
Humphrey motioned northwards with the coffee cup
in vague distaste. "You can run it down from that
much, old fellow," he told his friend remorselessly.

"But suppose the house is held in the name of the
old aunt, instead of your Miss Whoever-she-is?"

"I suppose it may well be: the old griffin's name is
Harvey."

Masterson chewed on in evasive silence for some
moments, his bulging eyes set dubiously upon his
visitor. "I still don't like it above half . . . I have no
wish to tangle with any more of your bobbery like
that affair at the Minnis," he declared flatly.

"Oh, that's all past now!—odd you should raise it,
for I came smash against that murderous major only
two nights ago, at a minor rout. We dealt famously!"

"Did you, by Jove," Masterson said without enthusiasm. "Glad to hear it. Well, I suppose what
you're pitchin' to me now ain't on quite that level of
desperateness . . . But Humph, you are poz about
this being the Italy ton's way of doin' things, ain't
you?" he asked morosely. "I mean, I know I'm no
town-buck like you are now, but I own it seems

damned havey-cavey to me . . . And I'll say this to your face: I'd never have picked you for one who'd risk parson's mousetrap, whatever the foreign fashion for it!" He hesitated, grinned shyly, then added: "When did this case between you come on?"

In quite easily overbearing his friend's lingering doubts, and taking care not to enlighten his misapprehensions as to the true purpose of The Idea, Humphrey was conscious that he was fortunate in his sole choice of assistant; for Dick was not only a game 'un, and up to all manner of kick-ups, and had been so for as long as they'd known each other as boys, but he also possessed a born-and-bred countryman's tolerant awe when it came to all matters of mode. He was thus more susceptible than some others would have been to the scheme which had just been (partially) put to him. Humphrey could read Dick's mind pretty well, since, before his Tour, he could see that he had been much the same kind of amiable clodpole himself. He now gave heartfelt thanks for that deficiency in his friend, saying heartily: "That's the barber! You're a prime gun!" Whereupon, clapping Dick's despondent shoulder, and passing through to the next room to pay brief respects to the Viscountess and Dick's sister, he then descended, whistling blithely, to the street again.

It was not very long before Richard Masterson began to regret his rash promise: in terms of distance, about half as long as it took him to walk from Clarges Street to Hanover Square on the following morning.

He had refrained from using the family carriage for the journey, or a hackney, for the cowardly reason that if his nerve should suddenly fail him at this stage, he would not be obliged to tell whiskers to

either their stern old coachman or some impatient
jarvey.

In fact his courage nearly did fail as he turned
north up Great George Street, and saw that ahead of
him it debouched so broadly into the Square that
comparatively few houses were built on the latter's
south side, so broad was the cut of the approach
street. He had vaguely been hoping to be 'unable' to
find the right house, and in that way contrive to cry
craven with a degree of plausibleness; now, though,
with his stomach a-squirm, he abandoned that last
hope as he approached the first entrance around the
left-hand corner of Great George Street.

Part of his unease stemmed from the fact that he
had not been at all sure of the correct attire in which
to pay this morning call. His natural inclination had
been towards his usual slightly starched, moderate
shirt-points, a good plain pair of breeches, and
top-boots—but, as he knew that he tended to favour
that garb almost always, whether the occasion was
great or small, wherever it was, and whatever the
hour for it might be, he placed no reliance on having
obeyed that familiar instinct now. He began to wish
rather desperately (as the first door was opened, and
soon firmly closed in his face, by an odious puffed-up
town butler) that he had thought to ask Humph
what toggery he should have put on for it; although
by this time he was also wishing, more desperately
still, that he had merely *told* Humphrey to attend to
his own hugger-mugger of a courtship . . .

Two more doors were closed to him, after his
initial croaking enquiry, by similar odious butlers.
He began to feel a shade healthier as he crossed back
over Great George Street, to try the remaining houses
on the south side of the Square. Three further
withering dismissals made him almost cheerful; but

then an old man with a rosy rural countenance opened to his knock and said: "You wants Mrs Harvey? Do ee 'ave a card, zur? I'll see if she be in—bide yurr."

A few moments later, the perspiring young messenger was led and announced into a parlour where two highly puzzled ladies were seated awaiting him.

"Yes?" the elder one said blankly, rising and stepping forward. "Mr—Masterson?" She lowered her frowning gaze to Dick's card in her hand.

"Er—yes, ma'am! Friend of Lord Begbroke's, don't you know—asked me to—to look in and see how you go on!" Richard stuttered, with his protuberant eyes cast down on the top-boots which, he was now tolerably certain, were not the thing at all to have pulled on for this present piece of business; though he was still deuced if he knew what were the right togs to have donned. Probably nothing would have served over-well, not for a smoky undertaking like—

"A *friend*?—of Lord *Begbroke*?" queried the younger female in trenchant tones; the one that Humph had formed the *tendre* for, he presumed, since the older one looked a trifle beyond the stage for a fellow to form a *tendre* for in the usual—"Pray explain yourself! I am frankly surprised, sir, that *he* can call friends with anybody!"

Poor Richard, agreeing intensely with this unloving sentiment, now found himself shuffling his unsuitable boots on the carpet; and removed his stricken gaze from them to a picture on the wall which hung at a safe remove from both the ladies.

The ensuing pause drew out in rather an agonising manner, until Dick suddenly made up his mind to get the thing said and done with; since it would plainly be bellows to mend for him if he stood there much longer letting the thing drag on in this style. So, all in a breathless rush, he gabbled out: "His lordship—me friend, y'know—desires me, ma'am, to establish if—Humph feels—since it's a matter of things bein' right and tight or not, as the case may be—Italian, y'know—I mean, if he's willin' to fix his interest he has to know first—well, that is, dash it!—he'd *like* to know first—y'see it's if the dibs are in tune, and the lie of the family tree and—and so forth! I mean—dash it—y'see—!"

He fell silent, not entirely from loss of breath and general over-exertion, but also because a certain dangerous glitter had now entered the younger one's eyes in a way which he didn't care for above half; indeed, he cared for it so little that he began to back off slightly towards the door; but to his dismay she advanced threateningly after him.

"*Lord Begbroke . . .* sent *you here . . .* to find out *what?*" she shrilled at him, her dark eyes now snapping terribly, and in a tone that would have singed the thorns from a Weald briar.

"The dibs—the family tree—must be in tune, eh?" Richard repeated faintly, watching her with dread. All of a sudden his overstrung nerves jellied, and he turned and scrabbled wildly at the door handle. A few seconds later, both the stricken ladies from whom he had so abruptly parted heard his sturdy boots hammering across the hall, leading to a mighty slam of the front door.

Mrs Harvey sank into the nearest chair. She knew that she was not the kind of woman who indulged herself in vapours, but nevertheless, for the next few seconds she seriously considered whether to make this an exception. "Who—who *was* that glumpish boy?" she managed at last to say, reaching for her vinaigrette with a hand that still shook.

There was no immediate answer to that question from her niece; that young lady stood rooted to the floor, her chest heaving mightily and with two high spots of colour in her cheeks which, under normal circumstances, Mrs Harvey would have thought very enhancing; and doing much to improve, upon those cross-bred and dark-ish looks which, privately, she regretted in her young companion.

"You have his card there . . ." Anne uttered at last, with ominous calm.

"So I have, dear, but what has that to say to anything? He must be mad—stark mad!"

"I think not, Aunt. He was merely performing a service for—for his *principal!*"

"His principal? But I thought you only had those in duels, dear, and money-lending: that sort of thing . . ."

"Precisely so! Lord Begbroke—amongst other flaws in his character—has a pronounced turn for duelling. But I confess that I did not know he possesses a *vicious streak besides!*"

Mrs Harvey, distressed as she was by the scene which had just passed, was a little further shocked by this intemperate language against an eligible member of the Nobility. She grew thoughtful, going back in her mind over the stray little bits of sense which had been hidden—like precious nuggets—amid Dick Masterson's address to them.

"Oh!—I do see what you mean!" she exclaimed a moment later. "It does rather seem, doesn't it, as if that young man was—well, asking some most improper questions at this stage," she said ingenuously.

This provoked a schoolgirlish stamp upon the floor, and the impassioned declamation: "What do you mean, *at this stage*? Pray understand me, Aunt, when I give you my assurance, once again, that I am placed at no 'stage' whatsoever where that top-lofty halfling is concerned! Oh, the *outrage* of it! Have you ever *known* anyone to hold himself on such a *revolting high form* as he does? Oh, I could *kill him!*"

And indeed she looked as though she well could, Mrs Harvey thought, seeing the clench of her two hands around his lordship's imaginary neck. Anne's were not rough hands, like her own pair (or, for that matter, as accustomed to wringing necks), but even so she would not have given a groat for the Earl's chances had he been present just at that moment.

Mrs Harvey now had several considerations in mind (not all of them pessimistic) which she would have liked to put to her ward, but a glance at her still fulminating countenance made her decide to postpone doing so. She merely counselled her: "Do try not to fly into the boughs, dear: you don't wish to shatter yourself for this evening, now, do you?"

Dick Masterson was left with little alternative than to hail a jarvey once he had quit the Virago's house; since his legs were by then wobbling all over the flagway. When one obliged him, and pulled over, he hauled himself hastily inside the vehicle and snarled out the words: "Clarges Street—and mind you spring those machiners gettin' me there!"

After journeying a hundred yards or so, however, and recovering a trifle from his shame and fright and breathlessness, his face gradually set in more vengeful lines. He poked his head outside and countermanded his instructions to: "I meant Mount Street, dash it!"

He found Humphrey upstairs, with his hired town valet still in attendance as he had risen later than usual that morning after keeping no less than four separate engagements the night before. Dick burst in upon the pair before the shepherding butler could get his name half-said, interrupting Hubbard to declare: "*Well now!* I spoke a bit too soon, didn't I, eh?—I mean, when I said it couldn't be as bad as that duel of yours! By Jupiter, I'd second you at a *dozen rendezvous* before I'd tangle again with one of your lightskirts, *damme* if I wouldn't!"

Humphrey, suppressing a languid grin, turned to the valet and sent him off. When that gentleman's gentleman, and the butler, had taken their pained visages out of the room, he said quietly: "You were successful in running down the ladies, then, I collect?"

"Aye, I was!" was the near-shouted response to that query.

"And—?"

"And the younger one—your jade, *I* collect!—ripped up at me as if she were *deuced Cleopatra!*"

Humphrey laughed his smooth, worldly laugh at this naïevety, peering in the mirror to set the folds of his neckcloth more to his liking. To own the truth, he was never loth to dismiss the valet who now served him; since, although the latter was well up to the knocker in mere London terms, he lacked the kind of subtle touch which his fellows usually possessed in Genoa or Milan. He, Humphrey, had patiently tried to teach him such perfecting points of his art, but the fellow had not proved to be readily instructible. Although this particular valet was quite young, like too many other Englishmen of far greater consequence than his, he found him sadly stiff-rumped when it came to trying out new matters of mode.

That reflection reminded him of what good old Dick here had just accomplished for him. "But you did what I asked you to, eh?" he enquired, carefully working the pin into the completed cravat.

*"By God I did!—God knows how!—I felt . . . God . . .
dreadful!"* Dick muttered, aware that these words
were a shade repetitious but speaking them from the
very depths of his soul.

Humphrey stood up, smoothed his pantaloons carefully back into their moulded shape, and said in a
bracing way: "Come now, Dicky, take a damper! It
wasn't really so bad as that, was it? And I'll have
you know that chit ain't my lightskirt, whatever
slum you like to feed to our servants, my lad!"

"Well, if she ain't now, then I'll bet half my next
allowance she never will be after today's work!" his
friend asserted, with due caution but also with great
vehemence.

The Tourist gave another indulgent laugh, now
stooping to examine the high polish on his boots
with a certain critical approval; for this town fellow
did have a certain touch when it came to the
champagning of one's boots. "So I am not quite first
oars with the lady, is that the case?" he enquired
with dry satisfaction.

Masterson choked for a second, shaking his head
speakingly from side to side. "I'd say she wishes you
the other side of Jericho—or else somewhere hotter!"
Calming down a little, he observed with genuine
curiosity and bewilderment: "Y'know, Humph, I can't
twig for the life of me how the Italy bucks get
leg-shackled in that fashion!—I shouldn't have
supposed enough of 'em would live it out! I mean to
say—askin' in that scabby style for a gel's prospects
over the dibs, and who her people is—are you *really*
sure you weren't jokin' me all the time?" he asked
gloomily.

"Oh no, Dick," the Tourist told him kindly. "Quite
the thing out there, I promise you!"

"Well, I know another thing—you'll never bridle

that one for lightskirt nor wife: whichever scheme is uppermost in your crazed loaf!" Masterson opined in frank terms.

"What occasioned you to think I seek either encumbrance?" was the immediate haughty rejoinder; but then his lordship suddenly turned a little pale, and he asked with a new slight trace of anxiety: "What kind of establishment did you discover there, Dicky? A mushroomy, shabby-genteel sort of place, no doubt?"

Dick Masterson, with a stoical shudder, cast his mind back to Hanover Square. Underneath his surface airs of rustic unsureness, Dick was by no means a clunch. "No: at least, I shouldn't think so," he said thoughtfully. "Their butler might have been a bit dowdy, but—"

"Oh, so they do keep a butler . . ." The Tourist's suave voice was now betraying a little more agitation. "And how many maid-servants?"

"I never sighted any when I was there but, yes, I should reckon they have a couple or so. The place was rather too spick for only one, lookin' back on it. But what does it signify if they do?"

Humphrey's face now wore a marked frown. He pulled at his under-lip, then shrugged and said over-casually: "Pooh, I don't suppose it needs mean anything . . . A *dowdy* butler, you said, didn't you? And worn drugget on the floors? And the old chaperon looking straight from a back-slum, I dare swear? And the house-maids all with that certain lickpenny, half-starved air about 'em?"

"I told you I never clapped my peepers on any damned house-maids!" Dick snapped, with a renewel of his former heat. "The elder lady appeared perfectly respectable and up to snuff. They both did. What new fudge are you pitchin' me now?"

Humphrey hesitated, then decided to share his sudden nagging concern with his sorely-tried friend. That concern led him to speak with a naturalness which harked back to the time before he had ever experienced the wonders of Latin society.

"Y'see, this is the lie of it, Dicky: the Italian town-bucks, when they've made their open enquiries through third parties, the way I explained it to you, well, if the girls ain't up to the rig then they cry off like lightning, see?—only honourable thing for 'em to do. *We* might fancy it should be t'other way round—but that's their ton, d'you follow? The only catch is—and honestly I never thought of this side of it since it first came to me to try out the notion in a harmless sort of a way—well, y'see the catch is, if a girl *is* up to the rig by some awf—by some chance, well then . . ."

Humphrey's mouth had now become a little dry, and he paused to swallow once or twice, tugging agitatedly at his fresh and beautiful neckcloth to allow himself more air.

"Well then *what*?" said Masterson, eyeing him now with a quite changed look of dawning compassion.

The Tourist bravely forced himself to pronounce the formal words of sentence: "Then the town-buck has to offer for her—that's the bit I forgot . . . If he don't, then some corker from the girl's side seeks him out and stabs him—or somesuch curst foreign thing," he concluded, with little sign of his usual enthusiasm for Italian customs.

"Oh, come now—stabbing!—doing it *too* brown!" Masterson rallied him. "Dammit, no!—never in Mount Street!"

Even the probable truth of this remark failed to evoke more than a wan smile from his friend, who now murmured: "So perhaps you see why I asked about their butler and maids and—and all that, eh?"

"By George I do!" said Masterson in equally hushed accents. "For with or without the stabbing—if that chit should turn out well-born and in full feather . . . then you're honour bound to be at Point-Non-Plus!"

Eleven

About a week after that desperate conversation, one fine late May morning, Lady Philippa was standing in the small garden behind the Mount Street mansion.

The ordeal of the Drawing-room now lay behind her and her sisters, together with the immediately following dress-party at Carlton House. Both occasions, though they had gone off well enough, had vexed her in one way or another.

She had supposed that, for once, her grandmama would be correctly attired for the Court engagement, with her passion for feathers at all times, but the maddening old lady had suddenly appeared divested of them just when their carriage was on the point of leaving. Feathers, she had explained kindly to her tight-lipped niece, were never worn by the *bon ton* at Court; she advised Philippa to remove her own, if the dear king was not to think her a perfect fright. It had taken several precious moments of delay to persuade her that this archaic ruling was no longer in force, having applied only to her own heyday of high plumage. She had continued disputing the point

even while the carriage proceeded, so that finally, in
a rage with her, Philippa had plucked some plumes
from her own head-dress and the girls' and wedged
them forcibly into Sarah's own toppling creation.

But later she had felt a twinge of remorse, seeing
the old belle looking pathetically about her for a now
mad monarch and her long-dead friends, amongst
what was by far the worst royal squeeze which
Philippa had yet encountered at a May Drawing-
room. Although she and the twins escaped unscathed,
she saw with her own eyes the clothing of several
eminent ladies of rank being literally torn in pieces
by what could only be called the mob.

And Carlton House had been just as bad; the two
experiences together had made her almost glad that
she were not the twins' age, and forced to undergo
such scenes again perhaps several times.

For she had now made up her mind unalterably
that this was to be her last London Season. Personal
discomfort aside, she felt it was not fair to her Papa
to make him stand the huff for her for yet another
year, when the sacrifice would be more certain than
ever to be fruitless. She did not blame Grandmama,
or her brother, or anyone, for her repeated failure:
catching a husband was just not her style, and it was
high time that fact was acknowledged and understood by all concerned.

However, Humphrey had not exactly made the
past week any easier for her to endure. Twice he had
sought her out for uncharacteristic tête-à-têtes, in
which he had pleaded all sorts of gammonish ex-
cuses for quitting town forthwith and returning into
Kent. She supposed that he was in some masculine
scrape—betting, very like—and desired to absent
himself for that reason. He had seemed quite put out
when she had refused to fall in with his wishes, and

since then his attendance upon his sisters and grandmother had become still more spasmodic and unreliable.

It was the realisation that these fleeting days
represented her last opportunity to make an eligible
match which had now brought Philippa outside to
stand contemplatively in the sunshine.

Like many a general before her, the sense of being
engaged in a final and decisive battle was having
the effect of sharpening her wits extremely; not that
she entertained any higher opinion of her intellect
than of her other despised qualities. It was her
private opinion that she and Humph were the slow-
tops of the family, and that the two younger ones
(Meg especially) showed greater promise; even if, as
yet, their superiority was too immature to show to
those who did not know all four of them well. She
wished so much that the twins would take well! For
if they only could, there was no reason in their case
why they might not—

She pulled herself up short in this impractical
day-dreaming. No one knew better than herself that
without the all-important appearance at Almack's,
it mattered little how well they might take at every
other ball or assembly, and still come to naught at
the end of the day.

Of course, it was an equal folly to suppose that
entrance to those sober rooms in King Street was in
itself an Open Sesame to marriage and happiness:
but none could deny that it had led to precisely that
on a great number of occasions.

She mused on in the garden, stooping to weed a
tub of sooty-looking carnations. Suddenly she gave a
little gasp, and straightened herself again with a
much brighter look in her narrowed blue eyes.

Probably there was not much that was truly in

common between the mind of Lady Philippa Freen, of Cornford House in London and of Hoadoak in Kent, and that of Mrs Harvey from Lincolnshire. And yet, a few moments later, Philippa was hastily washing the earth from her fingers and sitting down to compose a billet which was torn up many times before receiving her brother's frank but read finally:

'My dear Ly Jersey,
I feel constrained to express to you my sense of shock and sympathy at this vile and impudent publication by Ly Lamb. Lord Kinnaird acquainted me with the nauseous details the other evening at Mrs P's. How deeply shocking it all is! That such a work should obtain a prodigious sale is, I suppose, what one must expect from a work of libel in these times. I am very sure that all London feels for you and for the others so portrayed, as does,
              Ever yours most truly,
                    Philippa Freen.'

* * *

As it happened, the distinguished recipient of that note chanced to meet with her friend Lady Sefton at an engagement a few nights later.

It was a dull affair, redolent of what both those experienced leaders of fashion termed as 'die-down'; signifying the familiar period of late spring when gentlemen were becoming hard to come by because they were returning into the country, and ladies of all ages showing tell-tale signs upon their faces of the arduous past weeks they had endured.

Now, Lady Jersey was wearing a three-year-old simple frock dress, with square décolletage and a fairly low waist, and lacking the new Gothic flummery which she privately detested. "Ah, Maria!" she hailed her friend with relief, walking over to her, "This is *very* wearisome, is it not? Where do you go later?"

Maria Sefton, who was more conventionally attired in balconies of artificial flowers, Vandyked borders, and quilled lace, replied: "First to the Hollands and then, very late, to the Regent. I know what you think!—God help me! But *I* think that His aid is not needed any more in that quarter! I'm persuaded that *far* more harm could befall one at the Hollands, which still quite *seethes* with passion over the matter of the Posturing Ponsonby!"

"Oh, as to that, I had the pleasantest note from that tall Freen girl, amongst others. Calculating, of course, but well done . . . I think I may send her vouchers after all—what say you?"

But Lady Sefton had nothing to advise on that head, so busily was she now galloping off on a train of thought of her own.

"Sally, dear, you have reminded me—I myself had a note of *ludicrous* pretension a sennight back, from some woman in Hanover Square who once sent us some chickens! Ay, well you might goggle! It really was the most amusing thing! I laughed and laughed over it!"

"Did she seek vouchers for her *chickens*? That *is* a new come-out, even for us!"

"No, no, it was for some ward. You will think me unhinged, but I sent her cards, just to discover what the pair shall look like!"

"Oh Maria! One should not quiz people," Lady Jersey said with strong disapprobation, but with a belying twinkle in her eye. "When for?"

"Our first night in June. It is bound to be deplorable by then, and I fancied the chicken-woman might at least make it go a little."

Sally Jersey thoughtfully tapped her chin with her small fan, and patted her famous dark curls. "Then I shall mix the Freens in on that day also: the old belle is sure to do something comical. *How* I wish that Cornford himself would come to town, he has such elegance, but they say he sickens. The son is a rum touch who tries to be a foreign Tulip. The younger girls will dispose of easy enough—did you hear that Prinny pinched the cheek of one of them?—but I make no bones of saying the tall one's card is pure charity and a waste: she will never catch anyone now unless, perhaps, some April squire. Ah well, dear, it has been lovely talking again, even here . . ."

Her eyes left Maria's and shifted speakingly to where their plump hostess was sweeping the harp in a small saloon off the main room. "I suppose I must stir myself now, to thank this fearful mushroom for wearying me to death with her sad notion of a soirée!"

Hubbard was a man who had been in service in several superior town establishments at this time of the year: unlike the young second footman who had been out to fetch the letters, he knew the feel of Almack's vouchers without having to so much as glance at the paper or wafer between his testing fingers; and, of course, he knew the happy import of their arrival (even this late) at Cornford House. With a broad smile upon his usually rather taciturn face, the butler arranged the whole of the post neatly upon a salver and went in search of Miss Philippa.

Amid the general rejoicings which then ensued, Philippa suddenly noticed that their grandmama was not down yet. "I must tell Granny!" she exclaimed, starting up the stairs and leaving the squealing twins to decide between them such momentous questions as who would don which dazzling toilette for King Street; provided the other fond twin was not so piggish as to choose its near replica for that occasion.

Philippa knocked impatiently on the door and opened it, saying at once: "Granny, the most capital news, I—!"

She broke off short, for her elderly relative was not merely late dressing, as she had supposed, but reclining upon a day-bed, fully clad in her customary morning peten-l'air skirt and jacket bodice. Mr Grimes was stooped over her in the act of tenderly stroking her face with his hand; his other hand, which shook, holding a newly-singed feather near to her nose.

It was his appearance which disturbed Philippa the most, for his powdered wig was set askew upon his shaven head, and his cunning face was quite transformed with grief and concern. "Grandmama ... what is wrong with her, Grimes?" Philippa demanded faintly, advancing into the chamber.

"I ain't certain, my lady . . ." the old servant mumbled in tones innocent of their usual flummery, but his mistress declared at once in her familiar rasp: "Wrong, child? I'll tell you what's wrong! I am *wore to death with routing*, that is all that is wrong with me! This rascal thought my heart had stopped, but I have just told him that if *he* never contrived to stop it with all his tiresome starts, then a ramshackle night or two at Court shall not do so!"

Despite this stout talk, and Sarah's almost usual appearance, Philippa was still perturbed as she looked down at her. She had been aware that the old lady was not just herself, ever since the fearful squeezes she had suffered at St James's and Carlton House, but with so much else on her mind she knew that she had not paid her the attention she ought. Probably it was this bad conscience which now made her say with undue asperity: "Grimes—do you stop waving that *burnt offering* at her, since she is perfectly conscious! And Granny—I shall desire the doctor to call directly."

Ignoring the various pithy comments which this declaration caused to be flung at her head, she turned resolutely and went downstairs.

Her feelings were still uncharitable when she rejoined the wild scene in the breakfast-room. "Grandmama is ill, girls," she announced; and hearing her own repressive elder-sister tones made her more aggravated still. How typical it was of the 'Queen of Carlisle's Club' to elect this very moment of success to stage a droop! she thought crossly, stepping now over to her desk to pen a brief message to her father's London practitioner.

Once that missive was sealed, and away in the Penny Post, she went through to the housekeeper and prevailed upon her to brew a posset for the old lady. Armed immediately with some hartshorn drops, she then returned upstairs to see her again.

By then, the old footman was standing back from the day-bed with his arms absurdly outstretched in a supporting position, as the old lady took one or two quite spry steps about the room. It was plain that she was now making a recovery as she claimed, but Philippa had no regrets that Sir William Farington had been sent for; particularly as Sarah refused outright to have any truck with either hartshorn or posset, preferring instead the excuse (in her granddaughter's eyes) for resorting to copious draughts of brandy, of which she appeared to keep an inordinate supply at hand.

Now that she was easier in her mind about her, Philippa's thoughts strayed to how this latest development must influence their night at Almack's. One consequence was very apparent: whether her dear brother intended to be one of the company on that occasion or not, he would now most certainly have to come. With her chin set firmly, she went to find him and acquaint him with that fact.

However, to her surprise the Tourist was not averse to escorting his sisters to the select Assembly. Though he had formerly been heard to describe Almack's as the flattest thing in town; a place where a fellow couldn't wear ton clothes; and precisely the kind of mummery that was not in his line—those objections appeared now to be quite forgotten by him. Philippa stared at him suspiciously, recalling also the meek way he had agreed to accompany them to Court, and to Carlton House.

Of course, she realised that the former engagement had made few demands upon him personally, since his father had presented him long before then, at a lévée soon after he left school. But if she had not been still so over the moon at the chance of Almack's, and distracted by Grandmama, she might well have tried to probe more deeply into this strange complaisance on Humphrey's part.

The reason for that was in fact not a profound one at all; though it would certainly not have been made known to Philippa. For, ever since his last alarming talk with Dick Masterson, the Tourist had gone to great lengths to shun all functions where the maltreated Miss Thouvenal and her chaperon might also attend. The presentation of his young sisters, and the vast Royal rout which followed, had seemed safe enough in this regard; and he was more confident still that that Frenchified young miss (even if she should turn out well-breeched, by some devilish chance) was far below the touch of Almack's.

Due largely to some last-minute nerves and delays on the part of his female charges, Humphrey did not squire them to King Street until the doors of the Assembly Rooms had been open for above an hour on that evening.

Being now a man of the world, he was not very surprised that the twins should have been assailed with final doubts that their fal-de-rals were not to their liking, and insisted on changing them over for other toggery; since, after all, he appreciated that this major engagement might well afford each damsel her best chance of getting buckled to some poor nodcock before the Season was out. It was perfectly understandable to him that they would do their best to pretty over, as much as they could, those manifest glaring faults which, as their brother, he naturally knew better than anyone else. But he was quite at a loss when Philippa requested him to stop the carriage, when they were still just in Mount Street; urging him in an odd voice to have John Coachman turn about. He was moved to protest in stringent terms.

"*Damme*, old gel, what is it *now*? Don't tell me *you* ain't happy either with your rig? Good God, Pip, it don't matter if *you're* a shade dowdy amongst the stitchery sisterhood, now does it? It's *these two* who need to shine tonight, eh! Have John turn back, you say?—*damn it*, what for?"

To his even greater bewilderment, this sheer sound commonsense on his part made her nap the bib in no time, great tears rolling all down her face. Then she sobbed out: "It's too late!—as you allude—too cursed late! I don't want to go now!"

"Too late?" he echoed blankly. "But the girls are in prime twig—you need only glance at 'em to see that!"

Philippa gazed through her hot tears at the silent and round-eyed twins, then at her worthy brother. Realising that not one of them perceived the true nature of her feelings, she tried to render that more intelligibly to them by recourse to a lie. "It's—it's Granny ... I'm persuaded she should not be left alone yet. Humph, you go on with the girls, just set me down and I can walk back to the house from here—indeed I should infinitely prefer that."

"The old trout?" excaimed Humphrey, more baffled that ever by this diversion. "But that fellow Farington told me himself she's bobbish enough now! Anyway, she ain't hardly never on her own: I watched her in the garden this afternoon, takin' the air with that dev'lish odd footman of hers. Between ourselves, Pippy," he added in a knowing way, lowering his voice to exclude the twins, "I think that footman could be *something more* than just a footman to her! Been meanin' to say so before, but if you don't follow my drift I'll explain meself later, when you're at your sewing or whatever at Almack's," he concluded mysteriously.

Had he sought to revive her spirits in any conscious way, Philippa was sure she could not have responded. Now, however, his earnest absurdity made her smile through her tears despite herself.

"Oh, very well, the three of you!" she murmured into her handkerchief. "I'll go and sit and stitch, as you *all* deem very suitable for me, I collect!"

"No, Pippy, of course I don't!" Lady Ellen assured her at once. Lady Margaret, with a little less readiness and conviction (but a good deal more relief at the way this dangerous *contretemps* was being resolved) echoed this sentiment, and implied generously that her elder sister would shine down any mere sweet prettiness, of the sort which perhaps she herself would be lending the Assembly.

Apart from such unexpected delays beyond his humble powers to prevent, John on the box needed all his proficiency with the ribbons to guide them slowly through the crush of carriages in Piccadilly, before he could turn his leaders down Duke Street. And so, at last, their vehicle was swept skilfully into one of the few unoccupied spaces that was left beside the Assembly Rooms, and they hurried inside; uneasily aware of the habit of certain of the patronesses to close the doors against late-comers such as themselves. But Lady Jersey was officiating at the Rooms that evening, and she appeared to be in the kindest of spirits.

She came over to them at once as they entered, chattering in the light and bubbling style which, amongst her intimates, had earned her the soubriquet of Silence. "Dears, did you break your perch?—I know one breaks perches because it happened to my barouche in the Park, only last Tuesday—my lord, how tonnish you look!—but where is the divine old Sarah I so dote upon?—not jarred by the broken perch, I trust?—hello, dears, how sweet you both are to be sure! I *love* the gowns! Would you all like some orgeat first, or to be straightways dancing?—oh, by the bye, you girls may all dance the waltz with whom you will, we have a batch of very fine gentlemen indeed for you to take your pick—ah, I see old General Bramleigh is catching my eye, I had best fly over there next—*do* enjoy yourselves, we are done with the country dances now but I daresay you don't wish to bother anyway with such fusty steps—high rakers as you are!"

And she was gone, leaving the entire Cornford House party feeling as breathless as if they had uttered those several words of greeting, at top-speed, themselves.

"Lord, what a fiddlestick tongue . . ." the Tourist pronounced languidly. "Orgeat, eh? D'you want a drink of that stuff yet, Pippy? If not, I think I'll stand up with the odd high-nosed dowd and get the thing over with!" And, upon that note of resigned gallantry, he nodded to them and walked away, in his handsome black stockings from Florence.

The twins were then very quickly claimed for the dance which was just striking up; Ellen's partner being a gazetted fortune-hunter whose progress Philippa had observed, with wry interest, ever since the time of her own come-out. It took that experienced creature only a few turns about the floor with the ingenuous Nell to grasp that he was wasting his endeavours; and his handsome face then lost its spurious animation and became its usual vacuous self. While as for her sister, Philippa had never before set eyes on the arm which now guided Margaret—but its possessor's upright address bespoke a half-pay officer, and she hoped that Meg might have the sense to know that for herself. Watching her shrewd little face whirling by, she had few qualms on that head. Meg, whatever else, was sensible. . . .

With a renewed onset of the sadness which had beset her in the carriage, Philippa now made her way, with a stiff smile, towards the large group of sitters.

True to his word, Humphrey put up his glass and made a rapid selection of the sheep from the goats amongst the angelics yet to take the floor.

He engaged first a young lady in green and pearls, whom he had encountered elsewhere when masked and dominoed; or, at least, he was mildly curious to know if he was correct in thinking so. Once this point was established, however, conversation between them languished; and he passed on with relief at the end of the hop to another eligible, this one wearing yellow and pearls. In due course he performed the same steps opposite to red and pearls, purple and pearls, blue and pearls, and a rather bright pink and pearls. By that time he felt almost ready for some orgeat, and limpley repaired to the refreshment-room; his social duties now adequately completed in his own estimation.

He was aware already, by repute, that the fame of Almack's did not rest upon what one might eat or drink there; since apart from the sheer lemonade they called orgeat, the only other fare served by the invariably bracketfaced female staff was warm tea, and stale bread-and-butter.

The Tourist chewed a small piece of the latter, washed it hastily down with orgeat, and wandered back to observe the dancing. But then his bored gaze stiffened and widened. . . .

Simultaneously, Anne Thouvenal sighted him: and the amiable-looking personage in striped stockings, who was just then twirling her briskly in a Scotch reel, was very astonished to find, a moment later, that he was reeling on quite by himself.

Humphrey briefly contemplated flight; but saw that it would not serve, not in front of his sisters and, moreover, at a saintly tabby-party such as this. It would be the very sort of cut-up to get a fellow talked about all over town. So, grimly, he stood his ground, groping for his glass not for normal purposes of observation, but more as a kind of protective talisman against the furious and malevolent face now bearing down on him.

"You—you!" said Miss Thouvenal, investing that ordinary word with more venom that he would have thought possible. *"Oh . . . but I have such a crow to pull with you, my lord!"*

Twelve

From the first moments of their acquaintance Miss Thouvenal had always seemed to possess an alacrity of setting his back up; so that even now, resentment began to stir amidst his extreme apprehension. "Er, indeed, ma'am?" he parried stiffly.

"Yes—and put that silly disgusting thing away when you address me, *if you please*! *I* am not one of your *Mediterranean Paphians* and I dislike it *exceedingly*!"

"Eh? Do you?" he said in surprise, letting it fall on its long riband. "Why should you, dash it? Can't you see it's Classical?"

"I see that it is *disgusting*! All those shocking little lusty Cupids, crawling and twining round the glass part! *Ugh!*"

"Cherubim . . ." he murmured, regarding her with still greater unease. Not that he took real exception to this talk of quizzing-glasses, since, however vehement she was in her provincial view of such things, it made for a deucedly safer talking-point than what he feared she might have to say to him concerning the recent events at Hanover Square.

As if reading these thoughts of his, the fierce expression altered a little on Anne's features. Now she gave him a (rather bloodcurdling) smile as she continued silkily: "Let us not lose the thread, my lord: it was you—I collect—who recently despatched an *emissary* of sorts to my aunt's house, did you not?"

Humphrey ran a finger under his suddenly much tighter Oriental. "Oh, you mean that rum duke!" he stuttered finally, with a sorry attempt at a casual laugh.

"Yes, *that* rum duke!" she mimicked, with another tigerish smile.

He drew a deep breath. "Well, the fact was, ma'am—"

"No! *I* will tell *you* what the fact was—or, rather, what the facts are—and I hope you may find them worth the seeking!"

Anne Thouvenal, though her perspiring companion was now past marking such details, was dressed with rather more daring dash for Almack's than were most of her fellow-debutantes; not for her, evidently, were the safe ubiquitous pearls and muslins, and the single token piece of jewellery. Her dark hair, worn high as usual, gleamed with a long diamond pin, and a circlet of larger stones was around her throat. More diamonds still adorned a bracelet upon each of her arms. Her gown was of jonquil crape over a slip of white satin—but even that conventional simplicity for a girl in her first season was somehow made to seem a trifle ornate and unsuitable, so heightened was her complexion and so fierce the look in her dark eyes.

Humphrey would have been astounded to know that the young lady was in fact relishing this scene enormously. Although she really had been shocked

and offended at the time by Dick Masterson's hap-
less morning call, it had not taken her long, with her
own fair experience of Continental ways, to guess
which particular courting convention the Tourist
was attempting to transplant, with such sad inepti-
tude, to English soil. She also realised that he had
only done so in order to mete her out an ingenious
setdown, after her mockery the last time they were
together. And now, quite unbeknown to him, she
was determined to repay him in kind.

Smiling wickedly, she crooked an arm so that her
bracelet caught the candle-light. "Do you see this,
my lord?"

Humphrey eyed the bright stones in bewilderment.
"Ay, I do," he grunted suspiciously.

"What quality of jewels would you say they are—a
man of your experience would know instantly, of
course!"

He did not quite hear that last piece of banter, for
he was now experiencing the oddest sensation that a
hook was being inserted—only gently as yet—into
his lip. Forcing the absurd notion aside, he remarked
with undue loudness: "Oh, I should say by their
shine they are of the first water—I felicitate you.
Perhaps, for Almack's, not entirely . . ." He gave a
well-judged little cough. "But fine stones, ma'am, of
course."

But even this respectable thrust did not appear to
discomfit Miss Thouvenal in the least. And he was
still really in a state of total inner confusion, since
the full import of his own verdict on her jewelry had
not yet become wholly clear to him.

Anne now seemed to abruptly turn the subject.
"Do you recall, my lord, the other evening when I
spoke to you of General Flahaut, who assisted us
when we sought my father's Spanish grave?"

Humphrey drew back from that harshly smiling countenance thrust near his; for even he could now feel that he was being fast reeled in on that hook she had in him. "I—I remember that you let drop that name, yes."

"An *illustrious* name, is it not, to be at the call of a family of mongrel nobodys?" she observed dulcetly.

Now beginning to sense the whole, and with stark horror entering his eyes, he nevertheless made a game recover. *"If* one regards the friends of Bonaparte as illustrious—instead of infamous! Oh yes, ma'am, the name of General Flahaut is very well known. Once again, I felicitate you!"

But that final effort had cost him dear, and he stood before her breathing hard. Her smile curved more ferociously still as she murmured: "And the name of Marshal Dermithe Thouvenal? Do you know that too—when I *let it drop?*"

A violent spasm suddenly ran through Humphrey's tall frame, from top to toes, in response to that merciless *coup de grâce.* He said brokenly: "That—that Thouvenal . . .? My God . . . I never dreamed . . . I naturally thought you meant some common soldier . . . I mean, lookin' for a *grave,* damn it!" He fell silent, in a striken way.

Anne chuckled full-throatedly. "Marshals can fall in battle also, Lord Begbroke—and sometimes just as mysteriously as their men."

He pulled himself together, looking bitterly at her exulting face. "Very clever, miss—you have made me out a clunch as usual!" he ground out. "For even I know that a fellow that close to Boney would be well-born enough—at least by Froggish lights! And them barbarous stones all over you speak pretty eloquent of the fact that, whatever else, you ain't quite on the parish. So!—let's speak out plain for once! I collect you know well enough why I sent that gapeseed round to see you!"

"Oh, I do, my lord—to report me satisfactorily destitute, and from the gutter, so that you could rub my mean state into me and—and dash me down in that cruel foreign style!" Anne ripped up at him, in a moment of real rage which made her eyes larger and brighter than before.

"Just so," he admitted morosely. "Not that I meant you harm by it: more of a lark, really . . ." Sensing the acute personal danger which this last observation placed him in, he added hastily and with a tragic gesture: "But I was dev'lish wrong, wasn't I . . . and now, I suppose, I'm behoven to pay the price for being wrong . . . ah well, I always was one to pay my debts . . ."

He drew himself up to full height, stared out stoically over the heads of the dancers to the place above them where the musicians still sawed away at their fiddles, and declared resonantly over the sound of those instruments: "Very well then!—dash it!—if what you say is true—though I doubt it was the shabbiest trick!—I hereby offer for you!"

This style of proposal drew the interested glances of several ladies who were then in Hunphrey's vicinity; most of them, judging by their expressions, finding it while undoubtedly original (and delivered with considerable passion), a trifle lacking in appropriate sentiment. However, the response of the person to whom it was directed was straightforward enough.

A small foot stamped on the floor in a way that took even the distraught Hunphrey all the way back to a certain French public coach, two years ago. "And *you* have the temerity to complain to *me* of *shabby tricks!*" she told him, in raving tones which

hushed half the Rooms. Into that hush she announced
with an awful clarity: *"I would not have you, Lord
Begbroke, if you were the very last man on this
Earth!"*

A well-built gentleman, clad in the dark knee-
breeches and white waist-coat which were obliga-
tory at the Rooms (though in his case the latter
garment bore certain subtle touches which proclaimed
its wearer to be a man of discernment) had been
leaning for a while against one of the pillars which
supported the musicians' gallery. Presently, when
the monotonous sounds above him changed to the
tempo of the German Waltz, he strolled forward and
invited a lady to dance with him.

Philippa arose in a state of considerable distrac-
tion: for she had just been reflecting that she did not
care for the latest aspirant to Margaret's hand—yet
another half-pay officer, she hazarded; dangerously
older than his predecessors, round of countenance,
dashing-whiskered, and with a certain hint of
boskiness about his address which, whether he were
actually in drink or not, she distrusted to see around
young Meg. That young lady was not proving as
sensible as she had hoped. Ellen was now being
gallanted by a mere harmless fribble, and did not
appear to draw the concealed military in the company with anything like the same constancy as did
her twin. Philippa recalled now that it had been
thus with Margaret at several of the functions they
had attended: like many debutantes before her, she
was struck with Regimentals—to the point, it seemed,
where she could accurately divine their invisible
presence upon those male forms which now appeared
in sober black-and-white, as they mingled with the
true civilians at the Assembly.

The gentleman had murmured his name before he led her out, but with all this to preoccupy her Philippa had missed it. Now, as his arm encircled her waist and she forced her errant mind to regard the steps, he said in a quizzing way: "You have no cause for concern, ma'am, on that head!"

She gazed at him in astonishment, noting with automatic relief that although he stood no taller than herself, at least, for once, she was not looking down at a man. Following the eloquent nod of his head towards Margaret and her latest consort, she coloured a little and replied: "I assure you, sir, that I—"

"Pray assure me of anything you wish!" he interrupted in his deep amused voice, "—but I've now observed ladies like yourself conning my friend Webster there on more occasions that I can either remember or enumerate!"

She gave him a penetrating look as they moved together in the waltz. Matching his tone of banter, she said: "Perhaps you too, sir, are a *hidden officer*?"

"Not guilty!—though it's true I was until of late. Now, all that's put behind me. But as for Captain Webster, who so clearly perturbs you, I hope you will accept my word for it that his air of far-gone disguisement really does not herald the imminent ravishing of your ward!"

So he had taken her for a chaperon . . . But she was still amused, protesting: "Oh come, I didn't think that!"

"I'll go bail that you did! But Peter is so far from being a pest of young females that you would be amazed! Why, only two hours ago he was shaking like a blancmanger—the prospect of coming here tonight positively threw the poor fellow into trans-ports of terror!—hence his somewhat plummy order, else I should never have got him here at all! And I daresay you may well wonder what two bruisers of our sort are about, sporting a toe with you fashionables: but, you see, Peter's old mother had a way to the tickets, and we were both curious to see if all one hears is true—so here we both are!—a brace of the least promising beaux who ever entered these portals, you must think! But Peter Webster is as good a man as ever breathed, and no one has better cause to know that than I do."

She caught the change in his tone, and regarded him consideringly from behind her bright smile. She was looking at a blunt face, not quite handsome but neither ill-favoured, with a rather heavy and sad expression dominating it despite his humorous mouth and eyes. For some reason—although she was usually adept at what her brother was wont to apostrophise as 'ball-talk'—she found it difficult to find what to say to him; so that when the music stopped she returned dejectedly to her seat, convinced that she was now come to the pass where even conversing with a gentleman was beyond her spinsterish rectitude and lack of spontaneity.

Logically, this conclusion should have led her to apply herself with renewed zeal to the task of overseeing young Meg and Nell; however, it did not appear to have that sensible effect on her. Instead she sat staring unseeingly in front of her, the needles limp in her hands, until the odd little woman sitting on her left suddenly addressed her: "My dear, you missed quite a fracas then!"

"What? Oh . . . what fracas was that?"

"Over there in the far corner, by the lemonade room. Poor Lady Jersey did not know *what* to do! It was between that tall young man, who still stands there like a stock, and my niece," Mrs Harvey said calmly, her fingers busy with knotting the same red shawl which Philippa now vaguely remembered seeing slowly increase at several engagements since the Season began.

She looked across the floor at Humphrey, saying: "Your niece, ma'am? Do you mean that dark girl who is about to dance again, with all the—handsome jewellery?" she amended quickly.

Mrs Harvey's mouth twisted slightly at the sides. "Pray don't talk to *me* of those showy gems she displays! Oh, how I disputed with her over them!— and, you know, in the usual way the girl has *excellent natural discernment,* which makes it so strange, don't you agree? She is admittedly something of a cross-bred, from her father's side, but like so many of the *first rank of French blood,* she usually has real flair with herself: but she has insisted on wearing her dress jewels *everywhere* this past sennight! Now isn't that truly most curious?"

Philippa was finding the whole of this present discourse curious indeed; and opened her mouth to tell her neighbour that the male half of the disturbance was her own brother. But before she could do so, the quaint little rough-skinned creature ran on briskly: "The gentleman she is at outs with is a Lord Begbroke—a most worthy young man, I collect, whom she first met when in France. I believe he nourishes a serious *tendre* for her, for otherwise I cannot conceive why he should have made the most particular formal enquiries concerning my dearest Anne—or why they should now brangle in public. I feel that both irregularities must imply a certain *seriousness,* wouldn't you agree?"

Philippa's indulgent expression had changed considerably whilst this alarming intelligence was made known to her. Not knowing quite what to say in reply, at last she merely remarked in a dry way: "I know Lord Begbroke myself well enough, ma'am, and perhaps I should tell you that he is generally thought to be very high in the instep."

"Oh, I don't doubt it! *Extraordinarily* high, if you ask me, to send a *representative* to us at Hanover Square!" was the swift riposte to that intended set-down.

"A representative?" Philippa repeated faintly. Her eyes now began to kindle with some of the fire which had lately been in Anne Thouvenal's as she, too, now glared at the Tourist; who still stood morosely alone, shunned by all, near the refreshment room.

With a conscious effort she brought her gaze back to the placid shawl-maker at her side. "Er, your niece, madam," she said slowly. "You were telling me that she is partly French, I collect?"

Mrs Harvey set down her shawl in a businesslike manner.

"Yes: the daughter of Thouvenal of Ciudad Rodrigo. Do not ask me quite what that means, my dear, for I am not entirely clear—I believe it was a battle-ground where he distinguished himself. He was, in any event, a *very distinguished man*," she declared emphatically. "A Marshal of France. And when he died he left Anne and the other cross-breds *very well to pass*. He was also totally *un*generous to my poor brother's children, though I know that's nothing to say to anything," she rattled on in her flat Lincoln-shire accent. "Poor Alice—my sister—endured much for him, since whilst he was fighting for the French against us, well, the circumstance somehow became known in our part of Lincs—perhaps it was just the girls looking French, I can't say—but the village children would come and daub their cottage door with *Boney-lover* and the like. And after the war, of

course, Alice must listen to none of us, but set forth
on that witless search to find him. But do not run off
with the notion that my sister is ungenteel, because
I mentioned a cottage just then," Mrs Harvey hastily
caught herself up. "Or because *I* most assuredly *am*
ungenteel! Alice was always the ladylike one of the
pair of us—but life has not been easy for her. Our
Papa was the squire. Me, I only wished to be grub-
bing about outside, and I cared so little whom I wed
that, when Papa insisted, I took the parson's boy—in
truth, very largely because he liked fowls too!" She
chuckled heartily at this reminiscence, her fingers
now busy at the shawl again.

Philippa, though left highly unstrung by the general substance of this speech, could not help smiling
a trifle herself at the rare blend of frankness and
earthy cunning which she perceived in it. She was
amused also by the thought of such a person sitting
in Almack's, of all places. Mrs Harvey made the
plain ex-officer whom she had danced with seem like
a veritable Pink of the Ton . . . "I wish you and your
niece well, ma'am," she said composedly, rising to
gather her errant family together and bring this
preposterous failed evening to a close.

Mrs Harvey eyed her departing back with satisfaction. She was already aware, from a careful scrutiny of her Peerage book, that there was no present
Cornford Marchioness to stand in the way of matters; and was now encouraged to believe that she
and this sharp young mother-ish girl she had spoken
with might soon deal pretty well with each other.

It had been immediately clear to her that drastic
measures were required, once Anne had sent the
Earl to the rightabout so publicly in return for his
foolish pranks. Less resolute and experienced match-
makers than herself might perhaps have been

tempted to shrug their shoulders at that point and
let nature take its course; but not the famed creator
of the Spalding Blue.

For it was Mrs Harvey's experience that while
nature could sometimes be depended upon to handle
the various aspects of a successful union, and all
come right and tight in the end, she had learned that
there often came a crucial time when one very
definitely needed to step in oneself . . .

She waited until the Freen party had left the
Rooms and then got up herself to take Anne home;
since she now saw little profit in the girl's remaining
here any longer looking the over-dressed damsel she
did.

A few nights later, the Ladies Jersey and Sefton met
at the Argyll Rooms and fell to discussing Almack's
first June Assembly.

"Dearest Maria, it went *exactly* as I had supposed
it might! Those Freens were *unspeakable!*"

"Old Sarah, you mean? What did she do, waltz in
her hoops?"

"No, no, she could not attend—it was principally
that blockish boy of theirs—he came the ugly to a
fearsome girl who was in quantities of diamonds!"

"Diamonds . . ." repeated Lady Sefton, in a shaken
tone. "My God, but we are become careless with the
cards, Sally—I don't wonder that the Earl came the
ugly to her!"

"Oh, it was not on that head! No, the lobcock
offered for her, if you please, in the middle of the
floor, and in a charmless style to raise the dead!
Whereupon she refused him louder still! And, all the
while, the little Freen girls were seizing upon the
soldiery, with tall big sister glowering at them—so!"

Sally Jersey briefly contorted her handsome features. "Oh, it was all *hideous!*"

Maria Sefton sighed and frowned. "And what of my chicken-woman? *Was* she amusing?"

"She was *not!* A regular little country-dowd, who sat all evening without a thought in her head! I collect that it was her girl who wore the diamonds!"

Lady Sefton moved aside to allow a masked couple to slip past her, hands entwined. "We must exercise much greater care next time," she opined sombrely, "or else, the next thing we shall see at King Street is *once-a-week beaux.*"

And this fell prospect effectively silenced them both, until their throats were loosened once again with some ratafia from a passing tray.

Thirteen

Anne had not chosen to speak to her aunt of the outlandish proposal which had come her way at Almack's.

In the manner of many persons who become involved in 'scenes', she had very soon convinced herself that it had passed largely unnoticed; also, as her chaperon had been placed at some distance away at the time (and she still did not quite know how alert the little woman was), she had not felt obliged to tell her, particularly as she sensed that she might have a regrettable tendency to take his lordship's ridiculous words in earnest.

As none knew better than herself how completely and irrevocably she had severed her acquaintance with Lord Begbroke, she now formed a determined resolve to enjoy the remainder of her first—and presumably only—London Season. She set herself with renewed vigour to the business of dancing, laughing, talking, whistling and dining; attacking each of these nightly pursuits with an equal gay indefatigableness that Mrs Harvey observed with tolerant understanding.

The pair of them were at a ball in Ebury Street one evening when Anne was requested to stand up by a pleasant-voiced gentleman who wore a most stylish corbeau-coloured coat and black pantaloons, the cut of the former garment being suggestive of Scott's handiwork.

Anne lacked Philippa's practised eye for a soldierly bearing in disguise, but even so it was not long before she ventured to ask—in response to a polite question from her partner—if he had possessed a pair of colours at any time.

"Lord, does it show so clearly?" he exclaimed, with a humorous look of despair. "Yes, I confess you are in the right: my hobbling gait will perhaps appear more gallant to you if I explain that—at least in part—I came by it during a tiresome military journey from Badajoz to Burgos: if those names convey anything to your mind at all!"

He very soon apprehended from her catch of breath, arrested motion, and widening gaze, that his words had indeed meant something to her.

"Oh, sir—pray tell me—did you go also through Alcantara and Escorial? Is it conceivable that you knew my father in the Peninsula?"

He stared back at her, clasping her hands more firmly and making her resume the dance. In his now puzzled deep tones he murmured: "To your first question, ma'am—yes, I did pass by those towns in the 'Twelve Campaign. As for the second—what is your name?"

The sound of that name was of rather more immediate significance to him than it had been to Humphrey. He said something startled under his breath, and then, in a tone of flippant reserve: "To be sure, ma'am, if he and I had chanced to see each other somewhere at that time, you must pardon my pointing out that the most likely occasion would have been across my sword!"

"Oh, I know that, of course!" she cried impatiently. "But, you see, he was missing—ever since Salamanca. We—I—have been to all the battlegrounds of that march, attempting to discover what became of him—totally without success."

Realising that the trend of this talk was fundamentally unsuited to dancing, he led her to a long sofa against one wall. Seating himself on it beside her, he said carefully: "Do not get your hopes up, Ma'mselle Thouvenal. To me, he was merely the name of a distinguished enemy—again begging your pardon. I never knowingly met nor saw him—though I can well understand if he was lost forever at Salamanca," he murmured, his eyes becoming stricken and haunted as they looked backward in time. "For that particular carnage was—indescribable. You may take my word on that. I was with the Fifth there, under Cotton."

He fell dourly silent; reflecting to himself that what he might have described to her, had he been so callous, was the sight of several noble Frenchmen at Salamanca, each so disfigured by sword cuts that not only identity, but all traces of the human face and form were obliterated.

Anne passed a hand across her eyes, assuming a brave smile. "I am only half a mademoiselle, sir . . . Thank you for being frank with me. Of course, I knew really by this time that the chance was tiny but—" She shrugged, reaching for her handkerchief.

In reply to his further considerate, but very interested questions, she explained in greater detail how she had come to be in war-torn Spain two years before. Their conversation remained on this sombre subject until, during a lapse in it, she suddenly frowned and ejaculated: "Did you not mention that your slight limp derives only in part from that campaign? May I enquire what other misfortune brought it about?"

"Oh," he replied abstractedly, his mind still upon the past military matters, the most ironical thing!—I had both my legs broken, one after t'other, not in any cavalry engagement at all, but here at home—just because I was at outs with a drunken green head of a lord!"

To his no small amazement, his saddened young companion thereupon went off into whoops of mirth at what, for the life of him, he could not regard as an exactly humorous remark. "You—you must be the *curst dragoon*, then!" she spluttered at last.

He flushed a little, saying coolly: "I do not know who may have said so: though I must own to a certain reputation, ma'am, and one that has cost me dear enough—but, as I have grown very weary of attempting to explain to those who feed on such reports, they are commonly exaggerated out of all reason."

"But you are—I should say you *were* that same Major Hipsley: and you did fight a duel with Lord Begbroke?" she murmured, giving him an unfathomable smile.

"Certainly. At least, I would prefer to call it a duel *of sorts* . . . Now look you here, ma'am, you are acquainted with his lordship? Ah, small wonder, then, that you laugh at me!" he said ruefully. "I dare swear my lord Begbroke pitches the duel tale rare and thick, eh?"

"Not when I first heard it from his own lips—when he was running for cover in a French diligence!" she told him with relish, and her eyes no longer wet but sparkling with mischief. His head bent closer to hers as they talked on.

Mrs Harvey, picking away as usual at her shawl, deep in her own cogitations, and by now feeling thoroughly jaded with Society, failed lamentably on that occasion in her chaperonage; for not until Anne and the gentleman in the corbeau coat had shared two sets together, and also chatted animatedly between the dances, did she begin to take note of that marked conduct, and wonder if her ambitious schemes might not be coming awry in a way that she had not foreseen.

Philippa had made one tentative attempt to draw out her brother on the subject of his public proposal at Almack's, but this had been repulsed with some vehemence; whenever he became wishful of unburdening himself to interfering hags, she was loudly informed, then she would be the first to know of his altered desires.

So she had decided that it would be better, and kinder, to overlook that absurdity—since it appeared that no real harm had come of it—rather than risk injuring his wounded pride still more.

Another event which had influenced her to leave well alone in that quarter concerned a more ordinary proposal affecting her family: for Lady Ellen had been offered for by a Mr Paul Wollacott.

Nell had brought this great news to her rather as a young puppy might have fondly deposited its bone. She stood there with her tactless beaming face, in the small saloon at Cornford House, saying eagerly: "Is it not most *famous* of him, Pippy? Only think—he can call cousins with Baron Hall of Frogumpton! And I daresay he has at least ten thousand a year!—did you see his blue Weston coat, the night

before last at the Esmondsons? Oh, I am so pleased
to be offered for so eligibly!"

Philippa restrained her irritation and forced a
smile. "I am a little familiar with the gentleman's
expectations," she said gently. "And I believe it is
true that he is a cousin to the Halls—through two
marriages," she added with emphasis. "But Nell,
dearest—do try to grasp that a tonnish jacket, and a
handsome address to match, do not of themselves
bespeak a fortune or even a competence."

"Oh, I know they don't, but *surely* it is worthy of
consideration?—his offer, I mean . . ." Nell said
disconsolately. Her plump round chin came up at a
defiant angle. "He resides near Exeter, close by his
kinsman, you know," she added, garnishing these
plain details with all the consequence she could
muster.

"Yes, of course it must be properly considered,"
Philippa told her with an affectionate squeeze. "I
shall be writing to Papa presently, and will make a
point of referring it to him. Meanwhile, pray try not
to affect Mr Wollacott *too* much, Nelly! These are yet
early days for you!" she said rallyingly; though with
the silent hope that her openhearted sister should
never know the pain of late ones.

When she sat down to write as promised, her pen
dwelt first upon matters concerning the Dowager.

The old lady was now much improved, she informed
her son; adding that only last afternoon chairmen
had been summoned so that she could indulge a
whim to take the air in Grosvenor Square, accompanied by the faithful Grimes. Philippa had watched
her thus setting forth along Mount Street, with the
old footman stepping out stiffly beside the chair in
his frilled neckcloth and wristbands, and with the
sun striking faded colour from his ancient knee-

breeches; the whole seeming to an observer like a
perfect cameo from the past. Philippa tried now to
convey this scene to her father, although she knew
that the gift of word-painting was not really hers.

My lord's reply, when it reached her, was couched
in a far less poetical style. He stated flatly that he
had never heard of a Mr Wollacott from Exeter.
Although he was sure that he wished him well, the
notion that he attached himself to the House of
Freen was—he assumed—a style of Westcountry
jesting with which he was equally unfamiliar. He
adjured his eldest daughter to hint the fellow off,
and enquired in the same blunt terms if she herself
had been asked for this time.

The tone of the letter altered in a way Philippa
could not quite discern when he referred to his
mother's health. He seemed oddly . . . philosophical,
if that were the right word; and also needlessly
pessimistic. A sudden relapse, he warned in several
gloomy lines, must only be expected in a person of
his mam's years. It was altogether unnatural (in his
view) how little time had appeared to touch her until
she had become minded to go off on the town once
more. He now blamed himself for permitting such
folly, since to go raking at that age was plainly to
ask over-much of any constitution. He was prepared
to hear the worst at any time, he wrote stoically;
adding a rider here that he himself was now in high
gig, and Suddaby vastly pleased with how he went
on.

The missive closed with some grumpy queries
regarding the family's bills, which, Philippa apprehended, were now occasioning a certain restiveness
on the part of their absent sponsor. Reading between
his lines of old-fashioned and distinctive script, she
perceived that even the charms of daughter-less and

heir-free solitude were beginning to yield precedence
to a wish not to continue for much longer with proxy
expense in London.

She smiled with affectionate understanding of most
of these foibles as she tucked the letter away in a
drawer, the smile only clouding when she bethought
her of what he had charged her to do over the matter
of Mr Wollacott. However, in the event that task
was not so daunting—at least on one side—as she
had feared; since Nell had meanwhile luckily become taken with another town-buck, whose dashing
Marseilles waistcoat, it seemed, shone down even
the unfortunate Devonian's tailoring.

Humphrey's behaviour during this interval continued to trouble her.

Sometimes he kept his rooms for days on end, only
descending for totally silent meals. Whilst upstairs,
he could occasionally be heard declaiming to himself, in muffled but tragic tones which Mr Kean
himself might have thought not unworthy; at others
(though his sisters had no knowledge of them) he
would quit Mount Street in a kind of morose rage
and spend an evening not amongst the society of
Mayfair, but with the very different kind to be found
at Tothill Fields. On more than one early morning
he shocked the servants by returning with Blue
Ruin upon his breath, or the similarly distinctive
aroma of Heavy Wet; and, once, he came back
haggardly from the watch-house and Bow Street,
where he had paid a fine as one Henry Frampton,
market-grower, of Chelsea.

After that last escapade he grew a shade steadier,
and most of his engagements became respectable
again. But a certain brooding resentment was still
strong within him, as Philippa could sense when-

ever he sullenly escorted them to the Season's final
flings.

Guy Hipsley set out for one such engagement in a
highly thoughtful frame of mind.

Six months previously he had attained his thirty-
fifth year; only a few days after final confirmation
had reached him that his elder brother, Michael,
had fallen at Waterloo.

That near double-event in time had affected him
profoundly in a number of ways. Once the immediate grief of Michael's death was past him, he had
thankfully repaid Captain Peter Webster every last
one of the considerable number of groats which that
inestimable friend had staked him since he sold out.
He had truly not cared as to the state of the rest of
his affairs, once that debt of honour was requited
against all the odds; but, eventually, his man of
business had prevailed upon him to investigate,
under his own skilled guidance, exactly what his
sudden Baronetcy comprised in real terms.

The disclosures made to him, that autumn afternoon in Mr Twentyman's dusty office in Temple Bar,
still staggered him to this day. For Twentyman
appeared to have unblushingly enacted the precise
opposite of all Michael's instructions to him since he
went abroad. *Dispose of my Consols*, had come the
excitable word from Belgium—Twentyman had
somehow contrived to expand that stock of Funds by
half as much again. *Plunge on the Liverpool Ship-
ping Company,* another mess-room tip had commanded—Twentyman promptly unearthed some ancient hamstringing injunction which rendered it all
but impossible for a serving officer so to invest. And
there were several more such examples set before
him, in written form, of times when Mike had tried

playing wily-beguiled with his fortune, but been prevented by the deep little personage who was now reeling off a set of figures at him that made Guy stare almost wildly. "My God, Twentyman . . . I am transported straight on a magic carpet from Queer Street to riches, and I owe all to you!" he said in his straightforward style.

A suspicion of a grin had then for the first time touched Twentyman's pale thin lips. "Pooh, no, Sir Guy, doing it too brown by half—though I will say, there's not many as can put the change on me, be they nacky Cits or shellmazed . . . or hasty-minded soldiers," he amended civilly, and with a sudden remembrance of this client's own particular reputation for impulsive action.

Thirty-five was a good time of life to have one's rackety affairs in frame at last; and Guy felt no real qualm of guilt for this fortuitous manner of improving them, since he knew in his heart that if poor Mike could but come home again he would gladly be rolled-up twice over, just to see his dear face once more.

Thirty-five was also a good age to be thinking of taking a wife; that was what had induced him to do the pretty in London this spring—vastly irksome though that was proving, to a man of his disposition and experience. He had found it all but impossible to jaw away by the hour talking of nothing bar the vapid matters which appeared to fascinate the young females of his acquaintance.

That was what had seemed so piquantly different to him about Anne Thouvenal: to see a pair of lips as pretty as hers, and, moreover, to hear them speaking sensibly of such things as the Peninsula Campaign—that combination of appeal was very strong, and had led directly to the new Baronet's present

seriousness of mind as he set forth that evening for
Lady Lansdowne's, in the white curricle that he still
thought of as Michael's and not his own.

He had met and spoken with Anne on two occasions since the night at Ebury Street; and after both
of them he had been left a little more certain than
before that if any such creature existed as a girl of
rank and fashion to suit himself, then this one it
must surely be. As to her own feelings, he was not at
all so confident: sometimes, looking into her dark
eyes, he seemed to observe some teasing quality
which baffled and confused him; though at others
she evinced every sign of regarding him already as a
particular friend, and as one who could easily become something more to her. She certainly gave him
the impression of finding it an equal relief herself
that they could prose together of real things and
events, as an oasis in the frivolities which each now
realised the other rather despised.

He was astonished, on neatly feathering the corner
into Park Street, to see the Lansdowne house thronged
not only with carriages, but also with a sizable
number of tipstaffs and link-boys; it was clearly a
more major event than he had apprehended. One
policeman officiously held on to his match-geldings,
directing him to drive on to a nearby mews which
did not normally serve the Lansdowne establishment.

On entering the house, he observed that no less
than six footmen were reinforcing the butler, and
that great masses of flowers were set on either side
of the stairway. He thought the effect most grand
and romantic, and suddenly resolved to ask Anne
this very night. He knew that she would attend, for
she had told him so; and, indeed, he could already
espy her chaperon, seated with the others in the

inner room and working at her endless red stitchery. He fancied that the apple-cheeked old lady vouchsafed him a rather cross stare of recognition in turn, but was now far too on-edge to pay heed to her. For tonight, one way or the other, he would have done with this false world of ton parties, and return to a more genuine existence. He was now quite resolved to offer for Anne Thouvenal, and to let all present thoughts of wife-taking hang upon her answer.

Fourteen

*The Tourist had only consented to attend the Lans-
downe's end-of-season function under the strongest
urging from his eldest sister.*

He was now becoming distinctly reclusive in his
habits; and although his brief sojourn into low life
had not been resumed, certain of its aspects had
carried over into his everyday existence which caused
Philippa much unease—or, at least, would have
done so but for the imminence of the family's return
into the country.

A distinctive whiff of the beverage known in some
quarters as daffy now hung about her brother, at an
ever-earlier hour each day. Her concerned attempts
to reason with him on that tendency, and over his
comportment in general, had met with no greater
degree of success than when she had taxed him after
his curious proposal to the foreign-looking girl at
Almack's; she was merely reminded once more that
she was a hag, and adjured to mind her own affairs.

However, Philippa was not too displeased with
him as they set forth in the carriage, with the girls

and the old lady, for the Lansdownes. His demeanour
seemed fairly steady, and his eyes not noticeably
dulled as he inspected the other arrivals in Park
Street through the ordinary English quizzing-glass
which, she was glad to see, now appeared to have
replaced the brazed article which had come back
with him from abroad. Even so, she would not have
been so reassured had she witnessed the copious
last-minute imbibing which had taken place in the
privacy of his dressing-chamber.

The gin was working strongly in him by the time
that sets were forming for the quadrille. At first, it
only made him feel very calm: a treacherous early
effect which he had not yet learnt to mistrust in his
new preferred beverage.

For a little while, his feet seemed to glide with an
innate grace of their own, even through such a
complicated figure as the *pas de zéphyr*. But then,
unaccountably, whilst negotiating the less intricate
grande ronde, he stumbled and almost fell.

At once he felt Philippa's anxious eyes upon him
from where she sat; and, he was convinced, her
haggish attention was solely what caused him to
trip worse still, a moment later. Feeling rather
blurry then, he added to the consternation of his
partners by cursing them, far from inaudibly, as he
stormed and reeled to the side of the room, there to
fling himself down, all a-tremble, upon an unoccupied sofa.

As luck would have it, just at that highly precari-
ous moment for him he was granted the rare felicity
of seeing Guy Hipsley, his newly-reconciled old foe,
leading out she who was the sole cause of all his
recent afflictions and present embarrassments. . . .

The pain of that moment cut through even his
bemused senses and made them acute. He perceived

that Hipsley's elderly features wore (however preposterously) an expression which could only be taken for *romantic tenderness;* he saw also that the monstrous Thouvenal chit was smiling up at the fellow in a lure-casting style which went (as of course one might expect) beyond all decency; and his straining ears, even across several yards of crowded ballroom, caught that distinctive deep voice saying in tones of supplication: "Pray don't return me an answer in haste! I know that I have not waited near long enough to ask you ... but I cannot bear with this frippery capering much longer, and that is the truth of it! I shall go this week-end into Warwickshire—to my brother's place which is now mine, as I have explained. But if only, before I leave, I could know your decision, that would—"

But Miss Thouvenal never did learn just what summits of bliss, or depths of despair, he would then be plunged into, for at that very moment her encouraging eyes widened with shock, and she ceased to hear his address.

The first that Sir Guy knew of any sudden diversion from his proposal of marriage was a tight, clawing grip upon his shoulder. Though he was a heavy man, he was not expecting at all to be moved forcibly around in a half-circle, and so he yielded quite easily to that pull.

"You!—by God!—Damn you!" were the slurred but distinct enough words then flung into his face; followed hard upon by the noisy slap of a fist.

Hipsley took a step backward, his face still cast in its former mould of polite entreaty but now marked red above the left cheek, and slowly filling with a look of wildness which Humphrey had seen on it before; but not Anne Thouvenal.

He controlled himself with a mighty effort, spit-

ting forth the words: "Aha! Lord Begbroke!—and
half-sprung again, of course! My lord, I have to tell
you that I am growing very weary of this situation
with you!"

"And I, sir!—" Humphrey bayed, careless of the
gaping room, "am grown *dev'lish weary of you!*"

He stood there, swaying and glowering down at
the pair of them from his superior height, just able
to take in that Hipsley's usually tousled greying
hair was tonight swept into a fashionable Brutus,
and his powerful frame well setoff in a coat by Scott
with military-style braiding, together with moschetto
pantaloons. It came as a profound shock to Humphrey
to realise that this personage, whom he had always
thought of as a rough cavalryman, was quite capable
of cutting him out with Anne at least as far as
appearances went. He stared at her for a second with
mute reproach, until her answering gaze made him
look hastily away.

At this critical juncture a fourth figure came thrusting through the press of silent spectators. Even the
fiddlers had now ceased their scraping, one by one,
and were staring like everyone else.

Philippa ran to her brother, clasping her arms
about him and crying out: "Oh, pray, *no*, Humph!
For God's sake!—sir, I beg you will not regard him!
He is in drink!"

Guy Hipsley, unfortunately, did not at first unlock
his eyes from from Humphrey's to inspect the new-
comer. He said thickly: "I have little doubt that you
are in the right, ma'am—judging by precedent—but
do you kindly stay out of this! This lies between the
two of us!"

"But I am his *sister!*"

Sir Guy now shifted his gaze at this distressful
appeal, and his jaw dropped as he recognised his

Almack's partner. But at that moment the furious Humphrey—further enraged and humiliated by the intrusion of an interfering hag on top of all else—bellowed at Anne: "So you aspire to throw yourself away on this coxcomb after all I told you of him, eh, miss?—and tho' his regiment could stomach him no more than I could!—and tho' his purse is to let—and any gudgeon can see it always will be!"

"You *puppy!*" Anne screeched in response, darting at him with upraised fists. "He is become a baronet—and not merely a *useless expectant saphead*, but master of his own fortune, and with an honourable career behind him, and—above all else to me, he is a *gentleman!* I collect you are not even aware what that means! He is worth a thousand of you, you *insolent block!*"

But then, to her suprise, her passionate and quivering form was gently set aside from behind her, before she could rain upon Humphrey more than a couple of the volley of blows she had intended. Sir Guy released her, seizing instead with his powerful hands (and not gently at all) on Humphrey's lapels.

"You, my lord, are accompanying me for a few moments of your time," he told him with grating restraint. And indeed, the now inarticulate Earl was discovering that he had very little choice other than to go off as bidden with his newly-elevated inferior; or else risk gratifying the entire breathless company with the final *on-dit* of watching him being dragged across the floor.

Hipsley marched him out to the hall, rather in the style of a military escort. There, thrusting open the first door they came to, he pushed him forward into what was evidently the book-room of the house; not that either gentleman was much interested in that

since it was the privacy, and not the purpose, of the
room which they sought.

Hipsley closed the door and turned its lock, then
came deliberately towards him again, saying with
icy control: "I am confident you must share my own
wish, Begbroke, that this must be finally settled
between us. I am now well past caring whether you
are drunk, or unhinged, or whatever! since I know
that is your way when you elect to insult me!
Now—where is it to be this time? Paddington Green?
Wimbledon?—or have you a preference for some
Kentish ground again? And do you choose pistols
once more—or are you, perhaps, still in fortunate
ignorance of how to use them at the correct time?"
he concluded bitingly.

Despite that final goading question, Humphrey
had all at once become distinctly more sober in
himself. Yet he met the other's cold gaze squarely
enough, grunting: "Ay, Wimbledon, and pistols, will
both suit me well enough. The thing should be
settled, as you say . . . for more reasons than you
know . . ."

The elder man's set mouth curved very slightly at
that final piece of naïvety. "Oh, I fancy I can guess
the nature of those reasons: they shone from your
eyes, back in there, as plain as the daffy. Right,
then, Wimbledon it shall be. I will wait on you by
the Windmill, at four o'clock next Tuesday morning."

And, with those sombre parting words and a formal halfbow, the man who had come there tonight
with such a different declaration on his mind released himself from the Lansdowne's library and
strode aloofly out of the house.

The next morning there were two unexpected callers
in Mount Street.

Philippa had spent the whole of her intervening hours in bed in a state of wakeful nightmare, going back over and over the dreadful scenes at the Lansdownes and their aftermath. Despite this intense retrospection, she could only recall isolated incidents of what had occurred once Humphrey had pallidly rejoined them, so distracting had her general sense of burning shame then become. She could remember the absurd little countrywoman with the shawl, whispering to her inanely: 'It all goes on pretty well, by dear!'; and she remembered her grandmother's robust verdict on the ruined evening, expressed thus: 'Faugh, child, why repine so much on it? Gentlemen were always at outs in my day—I have seen ball-rooms *run red with blood* before a drum was scarcely started.' And she could also remember, poignantly, their hostess's face when the Cornford House party had finally taken their leave.

The Tourist had preserved a total silence while they drove home, despite the twins' steady bombardment of him with questions as to what had taken place when he and Sir Guy were closeted together alone. This innocence on their part had finally snapped Philippa's shredded nerves, so that she commanded them: "Not another word from either of you! Be silent!—or else you shall go home to Kent first thing in the morning, by stage like governesses!"

At the time she had really meant that dire threat, and it served the purpose of quieting them at least until they reached home. Then Humphrey had gone straight up to his rooms, and had refused to unlock to her when she timidly tapped on his door just before two o'clock; though she could still see the light of his candle inside, and hear the tread of pacing feet.

Now it was mid-day, and he had still not come down. She remained wanly in the breakfast-room, awaiting him, attired in the first garment that had come to her indifferent hand: a cambric dress from years ago, with a youthful flounce. She was just wondering if she ought not to make a more determined assault upon his privacy when the knocker sounded in the hall; even that small sound making her sleepless self jump up abruptly, spilling coffee over the table.

She was reaching for the bell-rope to have that damage righted when Hubbard forestalled her by entering, saying in a curious voice: "Madam, a young lady desires to see his lordship. I have informed her he is not down, but—"

The young lady he referred to had now walked into the room behind him, standing there squarely and looking very Gallic and full of sinister import. "Oh . . ." Philippa said faintly, sinking back on to a stool. "Thank you—I shall deal with it."

"No!" Miss Thouvenal interjected, once the door was closed behind her. "*I*, Lady Philippa, shall attend to my own 'dealing' in this matter, I promise you! I wish to speak to your brother, if you please!"

"And I am very sure you may do so, for all I care!—if he will not deny you!" Philippa cried out, tried beyond endurance by this evident continuation of the last night's scenes. "He has locked himself away from all of us upstairs!"

"He will see me . . ." Anne prophesied grimly, already on her way out to the hall again. "Oh— thank you, Lady Philippa—I regret the necessity to shake up your household in this manner!"

A moment later Philippa heard her voice sounding upstairs, and Humphrey's shouted and profane answer; then came the scrape of a lock, and a steady faint murmuring from both parties which did not quite carry down to her straining ears.

After a few more minutes, that same upstairs door was flung violently back on its hinges and Anne came stamping down again to ground level. Passing an apprehensive butler and footman, she treated the front door in similar cavalier fashion; running lightly down the shallow steps to board her aunt's chaise which stood outside.

Almost coinciding with that hasty departure, a gentleman was in the act of turning a pair of dashing bays round the corner of South Audley Street, and pulling them up to face eastwards away from Cornford House. He was alone in his curricle, with no groom behind. Once the team was secured to a tie-post, he looked back over his caped shoulder in a way that was a little furtive for one so well-dressed and turned-out.

His eyes narrowed when he caught sight of Miss Thouvenal, in the few seconds it took that angry young lady to emerge and regain her vehicle. Just for a moment, then, his face seemed to lose its healthy colour, despite the warm summer day. After the chaise had gone, with a deep sigh he climbed down and strode dejectedly over to the same entrance which Anne had left.

This time, Hubbard's starched address was even more pronounced when he paced into the breakfast-room.

"Er, a gentleman has sent in this card, ma'am, together with an *invitation*, I collect, that you might perhaps care to join him for a drive in the . . . he said in the *Park*. He did also explain, perhaps I should add, that he is fully conscious this is not the Promenade Hour *by any means*. I am charged to inform your la'ship that there is a matter of great importance which, he feels, cannot be disclosed to you in any more conformable way."

Philippa's one hand went to support her pounding forehead, as the other took the card off the tray and held it in front of her. She said: "Oh my God! *Hipsley!* But of *course* he is Hipsley! *Oh, how stark mad I was not to guess before!*"

This short speech was delivered in such self-forgetful, tragic accents, that Hubbard—a fervent admirer of Mrs Siddons whenever he had the opportunity—was moved to appraise his mistress with new critical eyes. However, he thought it prudent to pass no judgement on this spirited amateur performance, remaining gravely silent until Philippa recovered her countenance and asked him: "Have you—won't he come in, pray?"

"No, madam: and he was insistent that in no circumstances would he be prevailed upon to do so."

Philippa nodded distractedly, with vague understanding of masculine scruples at such times. Her hand moved up from her forehead to her hair—the latter as yet uninspected this morning but, she was very sure from touching it, of a haggish wildness. Casting a bitter glance at her gay first-season's day dress, she said in a voice of rigid calm: "Very well: inform him that I shall step outside presently."

When she did so, after a frantic few seconds of preparation, she suspicioned at first that she must be the victim of some hoax, since no carriage waited by the kerb. But then she saw Sir Guy's solid figure, awkwardly doffing his hat to her from where a white curricle stood past Audley Street. With her pulse beating tumultuously she moved towards him over the flagway, feeling like a ridiculous young girl in the old dress, and to be behaving in this hoydenish fashion.

A short time later she found herself being bowled round the almost deserted Park; although quite numbed to that solecism by what she was hearing.

". . . aware that I have a temper in me, ma'am, which has *always* got the best of me, and which I know now, after last night, always will! I thought I was changed but . . . well, mum for that—what's best to do, that's the question now, eh? I know full well that brother of yours won't cry off, for he's got too much spunk in him for that." Sir Guy tactfully refrained from mentioning what else the Earl usually had in him when he attended to an affair of honour.

"Oh, but sir, *you* could!" Philippa exclaimed, turning eagerly towards him on the seat, and with her blue eyes very wide and appealing. "Please consider it—I beg of you!"

Sir Guy smiled back at her, but with a certain masculine evasiveness that she recognised only too well, and which his next words confirmed. "Come, now, Lady Philippa, you seem a sensible enough girl—do you really suppose that would serve? I take it you know of our former . . . clashes?"

"I do: which is surely all the more reason to have an end to such mad folly between you!" Her severity was a trifle damped, despite herself, by his happy and unforced use of the word girl to her.

He gave a short laugh and shook his head, ceasing to speak while he turned the bays neatly round a tree-trunk near the Apsley House Gate. Regaining the Drive, he continued: "Though I'm not the blade I'm said to be, I have been out enough times to know that there are some orders of antagonism which will never be dispelled without being put to a final test. Dash it, I was publicly reconciled with your brother only a few weeks back, and it meant precisely nothing!

Oh, you're a woman and can't be expected to understand such things, but I do, and I can't for the life of me think how I can—"

Suddenly he cut his deep voice off short, and hunched a little forward in the seat. His heavy face seemed to grow much more alive, while she continued to gaze at it beseechingly.

"Jupiter! I *do* think I see how the thing might be done—if only I can bring it off! God, I'm so rusty now, and there's so little time, but—!"

Seeing her afflement at these elliptical remarks, he offered no explanation of them but murmured a vague apology and turned the carriage on towards the Stanhope Gate. After that he spoke little, clearly deep in whatever scheme had come to him, though when he finally handed her down at Mount Street he told her cheerfully: "Pluck up, Lady Philippa! I don't know but what we can still contrive to bring all about, and not too painfully! By the by, tell me— have you ever been abroad?"

"No, never," she returned in a daze, distrusting this buoyant change of mood and subject in the duellist, and wondering whether to make further, still more abject entreaties to him on Humphrey's behalf.

"Ah: so you don't know Spain at all then?" he said with a touch of wistfulness.

"No. Why should I, for heaven's sake?" she murmured wearily, wondering why Hubbard was so tardy in coming to let her in.

"No reason, I suppose . . . it's just that, well, you don't appear quite the bird-brainish debutante I find so many are! I confess I ain't got much time for the Polite World—seen too much rough life beforehand, I daresay."

"We think alike there, at least," she told him with

more warmth. "For I now find that I detest it! I should be blissful to live in the country for the rest of my days . . . Well, goodbye, Sir Guy—I know now it is idle to ask more of you than this, but *pray do try* not to kill my foolish brother—or be killed by him!"

To that singular parting salutation he gave an odd laugh, an equally odd deep look which flustered her somehow, and then he touched his hat and limped rapidly back to the curricle.

During the next three days, that smart equipage made as many runs out to Wimbledon and back to Berry Street, where Sir Guy rented his present temporary home. On the fourth day it set out at a much earlier hour than before, quickly and quietly and guided only at intervals by the light of a side-lantern. That time it had the same two bays in the bar but carried not one but three men; for that was the morning of the duel.

A kind of steely indifference to his fate had over-taken Humphrey as that day approached. One thing only was he utterly determined to be when he faced Hipsley once more, and so his stock of Blue Ruin had all been resolutely emptied away well short of the time for the rendezvous.

It was not solely his pride which had made him resolved to face Hipsley sober for once; but also, in part, because of Anne's last visit to him.

To his amazement, the shameless (though one had to say devilish adorable) chit had told him she would consider his recent offer for her 'very seriously' if he would only cry craven on the duel!

"What duel?" he had at first hedged cunningly.

The familiar Thouvenal foot-stamp was her immediate answer to that, followed by the advice: "Kindly do not practise your *schoolboy whiskers* on me, my lord! When two idiots *bruise all over a ball-room*, then closet together and emerge each looking *ten years older*, then it does not require much nose to smell a duel in the air!"

"Ten years older, you say, eh?" he had mused with an air of innocence. "That would make your *new baronet* appear about eighty-ish, I would judge! I wonder that you should care a rush how old he looks—unless, of course, you are finally set on acquiring yourself an *English father*, ma'am!"

The exchange had deteriorated sharply once that point was reached, and even more unforgivable words had been freely vouchsafed by both parties. Only after Anne was gone, and it dawned on him that it was now clearly impossible for the two of them to bandy words ever again, had a mood of most surprising melancholy overtaken him: a mood more acute than the one which had driven him to Tothill Fields, and different in character from that. It remained with him still, and had compensated for the absent liquor in making him feel a genuine indifference to the morrow's outcome.

That new sense of fatalism also made it possible for him to sleep as soundly as usual for the first few hours after darkness fell. Then, as instructed, Grimes came to his chamber and rousted him up.

He had besought the old footman to act for him for two reasons: Dick Masterson, when approached, had declined in the most positive terms to repeat that office. He had then been puzzled to find himself an alternative second; eventually turning to Grimes since, for all the latter's eccentric ways, he, like his mistress, had grown up in an age when such encounters were commonplace, and he still thought very lightly of undertaking a midnight bolt out to Wimbledon for such a purpose.

Humphrey checked his pistol in the candlelight, paying wry attention to the trigger mechanism. Then the two of them stole downstairs and went out to where horses stood ready-tied, with leather bags over their hoofs to deaden the sound. Once the town streets, and the Watch, were left well behind, they dismounted in the Park and removed the mufflers; then turned the prads southward over the silvery grass, urging them to a gallop between the black trees, under scudding clouds and a very clear moon.

Fifteen

Philippa paid little heed to the fact that her brother was once again absent from the breakfast-table. For all her sympathy and attention, that morning, was bespoken by the sorrowful twins.

To their utter chagrin, neither young lady had received an eligible offer throughout the time while she was in London; and, now that they were about to return to Kent, this devastating fact could no longer be ignored or denied. "Oh, Pip, I had such hopes of Lord Trevisick!" mourned Ellen. "And *I* had every reason to depend on my Honourable but *treacherous* Mr Wallace!" put in Margaret in her usual competitive style.

Philippa smiled at them patiently. "Come now—finish up your bread and butter," she told them on a purposely prosaic note. "And console yourselves that only a few receive good offers in their come-out year—you are both still far too young to be looking for serious *partis*, but now that you have acquired a little gloss, next year may well be another story."

Lady Margaret here began to murmur through her breakfast words to the effect that her eldest sister was living proof of the falsity of that theory, but Ellen cut hastily across this by asking: "Pippy, shall you escort us again next Season, like this?"

"No, dear, I don't think I shall."

"Whyever not?"

"Because, chucklehead, she has given up!" declared the irrepressible Margaret.

"Well, yes, if you must know I have!" Philippa burst out dangerously. "I am sick and tired of men and their endless follies and foibles! I take leave to doubt if there is a sane or even sensible one on this Earth! They are all bottomlessly selfish and—and bent upon self-destruction! Consider our brother upstairs and Sir Guy Hipsley, for instance! Neither one will rest easy until he sees the other put on a hurdle! What can be done with such absurd creatures? *Nothing!*"

This was received as a rank heresy by the disgruntled twins. A babel of disputation broke about her head, but, only a few seconds later, her opinions were dramatically confirmed by no less a personage than Hubbard.

That smooth town servant now came stumbling into the room, wild-eyed and dishevelled, crying: "Miss Philippa! Oh, come quick, madam! His lordship is come home—horizontal!"

Sir William Farington stood back from the bedside with a rather affected sigh.

Unlike the anonymous physician who had attended the duel itself, Sir William was not at all accustomed to extracting lead from his patients' bodies. But his absent colleague had made a mull of a fairly simple business, and Sir William's professional instincts had overborne his nice scruples. However, he now said suavely: "That should render him more comfortable, Lady Philippa, and I foresee no complications. But if further treatment should be needed, then I think I must ask you to seek it elsewhere ... How does your father go on now? I ran across Knight in Grosvenor Street last month and, while discussing cases, he told me that he has contrived to *pull him through*. Capital! I suppose you will soon be with him again, once this case of, er, accidental injury can travel, eh? Well, I'd best look in on the old lady while I am here: I collect that no one has shot *her* of late? 'Servant, Begbroke."

"Prosy beggar!" said the Tourist once the door was closed, but he was grinning broadly on his bed.

"Oh, Humphy, what *am* I to do with you?" Philippa cried softly, seating herself beside him with careful tenderness. "Does the leg hurt *very* much?"

"Like the Devil, Pip," he admitted with a wince. "But *damme*, what artistry, eh? I've been lessoned by a complete hand! Y'know, that fellow could have killed me like winking!" He snapped his fingers above the counterpane in illustration, smiling happily into her perplexed face. "Oh, he's a right 'un! Fancy, he showed me a sketch afterwards of just where he'd reckoned to burn me—and, by God, he'd done it to the inch on his plan!—just enough to put me down without touchin' the bone. He practised out at the Common for hours on end so as to be able to do it so exact! Ain't that famous, eh? And do you know what he said to me afterwards?—he said: 'You're still one leg up on me, my lad!' Oh, a *complete* hand!"

"You—you didn't shoot him, then?" she asked with a sudden sharp anxiety.

His grin became a trifle abashed. "Lord, no! I hit the dashed windmill! That's more my touch for a target—unlike old Guy . . . Oh, I was forgetting, Pip—he wants to see you below when you have a moment."

"Sir Guy is here now? And wants to see me? Why should he?" she said slowly.

A glint showed for an instant in her brother's eye, sliding away before she was sure it was there. "Who knows?" he said casually.

"I suppose it is to apologise for hurting you, though that seems . . . unnecessary. I must say I think he has somehow done you a great deal of good!"

Humphrey's face became reflectively serious for a moment. "He has, Pip. All manner of sourness inside me came out through that bullet-hole, believe you me! But even so, I ain't so sure I'm just what's on his mind this minute!"

She eyed him distrustfully, made sure that he was comfortable, and proceeded downstairs. There, to her astonishment, she saw not only Sir Guy but also Anne Thouvenal, both in close and earnest conversation near the vestibule.

The dark-looking girl smiled at her as she came down to them, saying: "Lady Philippa, is it too soon for me to console the wounded hero? You will be wondering how I know already of what has happened, but your funny old footman brought me his message without delay. And I hear now, from his adversary no less, that he is vastly improved for being shot! That seems to me a most extraordinary consequence —though in his case I can believe almost anything! Shall I go up?"

"Yes, of course, he is perfectly stout . . . Sir Guy, I believe that you wish to speak with me?"

Perhaps it was as well that Philippa, during the very important talk which then ensued, had not overheard the Baronet's previous whispered words

in the hall; for although they had been a shade
enigmatic at times, she was by no means too slow to
have grasped their implication.

"Oh ... you!" Anne had said awkwardly, when
Hubbard first admitted her.

"Yes, me," Sir Guy answered in a dry way. "So
here you are come to see him *again*, I collect?"

"Yes: but how did you know I came here before?"

"For the simple reason that I was just arriving in
my carriage when you stepped—or rather ran—
outside: full of *spurned enragement* !" he added with
an attempt at lightness.

Anne studied his inscrutable expression for a moment. "You are no fool, Sir Guy," she observed
finally.

"I hope not, ma'am! Tho' it was not too difficult a
case to judge. It seemed to me likely that you might
approach one or t'other of us with your—proposition!"
he told her playfully.

Her face flamed despite his tact. "And so you knew
then ... that I did not love you?"

He shrugged, studying his Hessians upon the equal
polish of the hall floor. "I was not certain until
Begbroke told me the whole this morning—after our
contest, when we became so harmonious! But once I
saw you leaving the boy that day, and in such high
dudgeon, I was pretty sure I had reached Point-Non-
Plus with you. Go on, you baggage!—go up to him
when Philippa comes down—here she is now! I desire a private word with her," he said blandly.

And, once that privacy was attained, in the Pink
Saloon, he lost little time in possessing himself
firmly of both Lady Philippa's hands.

"No, my love, I most decidedly do *not* wish to
speak now of your estimable brother!" he said in
response to her first puzzled question. This style of

answer, and his general address, made her open her
blue eyes very roundly at him, and decide to listen
for a while rather than continue at such sadly con-
fusing cross-purposes.

Sir Guy observed this sensible compliance with
satisfaction, drawing her a little closer to him.
"Philippa—did you mean what you said to me about
being sick to death of town life?"

"My God, yes!" was the immediate and unequivocal
reply.

"And do you suppose that you would *remain* weary
of it?—even, say, if buried indefinitely in Warwickshire? For what I have in mind to do with the rest of
my mis-spent existence is merely to live at my late
brother's house, and farm and farm and farm! For,
alas, I am a mere clodpole at heart—though I have
taken a long time to know it."

She pressed his broad chest away from her a little
and looked into his eyes, her own beginning to
twinkle. "So this is a *rustic proposal*, sir?"

"If you can contemplate taking no more than a
mere baronet—yes," he said seriously. "I know that I
am not a great catch for you, and—"

"And have such a *fearful reputation*?" she sup-
plied, shaking her head sorrowfully. "Which includes
a distressing tendency to form the most unsuitable
attachments for much-too-young ladies of French
lineage? *Cloddishly* ignoring the very plain fact that
she is quite as besotted with my unspeakable brother
as he is with her? Oh, yes, I know all that well
enough, you—you darling! As for your baronetcy,
you are wrong to think I turn up my nose at it: I
simply don't care a fig about it, one way or the other.
However, Papa does care for such things, since he
enjoys his consequence in the old way. I'm sure it
will answer well enough to bring him about to—to

us. And he shall like Anne for Humphy too, because she stems from a Marshal of France, and Papa always dotes on Continentals of condition. While as for your habitual duelling, and other *penchants*, well, I daresay they will prove fairly controllable, in the fastness of Warwickshire!"

Now it was Guy Hipsley's turn to widen his eyes and his lips at this calm and comprehensive summary; then, with a great bass roar of laughter, which almost drowned her own happy peal, he folded her in his arms.

As was only to be expected from the younger pair upstairs, their similar exchange had been conducted with far less stylishness, despite some ingenious (and typically unscrupulous) advice which the Baronet had bestowed upon his defeated adversary while they were returning together from the rendezvous.

Philippa—and, indeed, Doctor Farington—would have been alarmed to see what a sharp and sudden relapse the Tourist had suffered by the time that Anne entered his chamber. He lay there supine, peering up at her in a most pathetic manner and sighing faintly: "Pip, old gel, is that your sweet face I see before me once more?"

The trenchant opening words, rehearsed while she was mounting the stairs, froze on Miss Thouvenal's tongue. Instead she murmured aghast: "No—it's Anne! Oh, Humphrey, you go on *much* worse than they said you do! Why was I not warned!" She bustled closer, exclaiming in still more shaken accents: "How on fire your brow feels! And what a colour you are! Oh, I must fetch some water to cool you!"

The Tourist smiled with satisfaction as she dashed

briefly away. It had been a dead bore, keeping one's head stuffed under the covers ever since Philippa had left him, but good old Guy had been poz it was the right way to rig the snare, and so it appeared. What a prime gun the man was! How he had ever come to cuffs with such a Goer as the Baronet now seemed a perfect mystery to him.

He suffered his brow to be bathed, emitting one or two more groans. Then, judging this to be the moment to make a recovery of sorts, he caught hold of one of the ministering wrists and murmured: "Ah, dearest Anne, the pain is not to be damped in that quarter, alas . . ."

"Isn't it?" she grunted, noting, with a rush of suspicion, that his face had already almost paled to its normal healthy tinge though she had scarcely moistened it yet.

"No: for it is in my heart," he declared, coming up romantically on to one elbow.

She slowly regained an upright position, her hand clenching on the soaked handkerchief, beginning to quiver all over with the usual Thouvenal intensity. "You—you—you *fiend!* You're *hoaxing me!*"

"No I ain't! Well—maybe a trifle—but I do love you, Anne! Dev'lishly! The thing came to me at Wimbledon, when old Guy was about to pack me off to Hades—as I thought. Just before we both fired, I said to meself: *deuced shame about that pretty little half-breed chit—won't ever be able to get buckled to her now!* And y'know what?—I didn't care a rush then whether his ball took me off or not. That's the *truth,* I tell you! What are you smirkin' at a fellow like that for? Dash it, you might have the grace to take a fellow's proposal in earnest, when he's spat the thing out twice over! What *more* d'you want?— once at Almack's, now again here, and still you—!"

"Yet another eloquent appeal may turn the trick, my lord," she interposed demurely, stooping to kiss his aggrieved lips. "If you will ask me once more, at my mother's house in Lincolnshire," she added, with the first look of shyness on her face that he had ever seen there.

A day or so later, Mrs Harvey was sitting down in her drawing-room at Hanover Square to write to that very same direction; communicating first to her sister, naturally enough, the important matters that were upon her mind before proceeding to the more trivial. She began:

'Dst. Alice,

'This is just a line in haste to request you *most urgently* to direct Higgins to separate the white-splash pullet (he will know the little lady I have in mind) from the old long-backed cock bird. The latter old chap is too impetuous for her by far, and, in any event, I am now sure their children would look dreadfully. I should have had the sense to know it before I put them together. It has been on my mind all these past weeks away from home, on and off, but now she will almost be laying again and so *they must be disunited*. I know I may depend on you to see my wishes carried out in this *most vital regard*. We shall return very soon, but that could well prove *too late*. Also, pray cajole Higgins to repair my large end-house (he knows which I mean, I have reminded him of it for ever), lest the badgers break in again, as they did last year, just when I had it so provokingly full of young ones.

'Speaking of the young, Anne has fixed the interest of a Lord Begbroke—a personable young man of the First Stare, as they say in these parts. I hope you shall be pleased . . .'